My Story

THE
SWEEP'S
BOY

Jim Eldridge

To Lynne, my inspiration, as ever.

While the events described and some of the characters in this
book may be based on actual historical events and real people,
Will Reed is a fictional character, created by the author, and his
story is a work of fiction.

Scholastic Children's Books
Euston House, 24 Eversholt Street,
London, NW1 1DB, UK
A division of Scholastic Ltd
London ~ New York ~ Toronto ~ Sydney ~ Auckland
Mexico City ~ New Delhi ~ Hong Kong

Published in the UK by Scholastic Ltd, 2010

ISBN 978 1407 11114 8

Printed and bound in the UK by Bookmarque Ltd, Croydon, Surrey

2 4 6 8 10 9 7 5 3 1

Chapter one

"Get off! Get off! It's mine!"

I was coming out of the wash-house when I heard a girl's voice yelling and screaming. Everything was in that yell: fear, anger, hunger, desperation.

I ran to the corner of the building and saw Billy Mangle, the worst thug and bully in the workhouse, struggling with a small girl. As he swung her round I saw her face. It was Milly Perkins. She was six years old and thin as a rake. She was holding on to a piece of bread, and Mangle was trying to get it off her, tugging at the bread with one hand and banging on Milly's fingers with the knuckles of his other hand. But Milly wasn't giving it up that easily. She gripped that piece of bread as if her life depended on it.

I hesitated. I wanted to run to help Milly, but like most of the kids at the workhouse I'd been beaten up by Mangle and his gang of bigger boys more than once. If I went to help her, I'd suffer. The sensible thing to do was go back into the wash-house and pretend I hadn't seen anything.

Then Mangle punched Milly hard in the face, and she

fell backwards onto the cobbles of the yard, blood pouring out of her nose. But still she hung on to that piece of bread. Mangle swore and kicked her, his heavy boot thudding into her side, and she yelled out in pain.

That was too much.

"Leave her alone!" I shouted, and began running towards them.

Mangle turned, his face showing fear that he might have been caught by someone important. Then he saw it was me and his expression changed to a sneer.

"You!" he said. "What are you going to do about it?"

I should have stopped then. Turned and just run off. But I knew that as he'd seen me, he'd find me and bash me anyway and warn me to keep my mouth shut. And the sight of Milly lying on the ground, crying, her face messed with blood, but still hanging on to that piece of bread, filled me with such anger. The memories of all the years he'd beaten me and the other smaller kids overwhelmed me. I leapt at him and began punching and kicking him.

Mangle was too shocked to react at first. No one did this to him. I managed to get a few punches in, but then he shook his head, let out a snarl and aimed his fist at my face. By then I was seeing and feeling nothing but hatred for Mangle. I grabbed hold of him around his neck with one hand, hung on tight so he couldn't get a proper swing at me, and hit and hit him with my other hand.

"Get off me!" he yelled.

I felt him claw at the skin of my face with one of his hands, his thumb jabbing at me, trying to poke me in the eyes. I moved my head so my mouth was near his hand, then I sank my teeth hard into his thumb.

Mangle screamed.

Through my anger I heard the sounds of running feet and shouting, kids yelling, and an adult shouting angrily, "Stop that!"

It was Abel Drutt, the Master of the workhouse, and an even bigger bully than Mangle.

But I didn't stop. I bit harder and carried on punching Mangle. Then I heard a swishing sound, and a sudden pain like a red-hot poker tore across the back of my neck. It was Abel Drutt's cane, the weapon he liked to beat us children with.

Drutt lashed at me with the thin vicious stick, cutting me even through my clothes. If I'd had thicker clothing it might have saved me from his cane, but in the workhouse we only wore the cheapest and thinnest.

"Get off him!" raged Drutt as he cut at me.

The pain brought me to my senses. I had to get away from here or they'd beat me badly, possibly kill me, for what I had done.

I let go of Mangle and ducked down under Drutt's next blow, and then began to run. But where could I go?

Already Drutt was gathering the bigger boys, Mangle's gang, and ordering them to stop me.

"Get him!" he shouted.

I ran blindly. All I knew was I had to get away. I saw that three of the bigger boys had already taken up position by the main gate, so there was no way out for me that way. Another two were standing by the smaller gate that led out to the back lane. The only routes out of the workhouse yard were cut off.

I thought quickly, driven by fear. If I ran inside the building they would follow me and find me. I'd be trapped.

There was only one possible way out: over one of the high red-brick walls that surrounded the workhouse yard.

Desperately I ran to the nearest wall, looking for anywhere there might be bricks jutting out a bit, or gaps where I could push my fingers between the bricks to get a handhold. I had always liked climbing up rickety surfaces, but this was different. Now I'd be climbing for my life.

The bigger boys were moving towards me now. I could sense that my attack on Mangle, especially biting his thumb, had made them wary of me. I expect they were worried that I might have gone mad and might attack and bite them. But Drutt was urging them on towards me, waving his cane.

"Get him!" he shouted. "There are enough of you!"

This seemed to give the bigger boys courage, and they started to move towards me with more purpose. They fanned out into a big circle and began to close in. Mangle had joined them, and he had an evil and vengeful scowl on his face as he looked at me. I knew then that climbing the wall was my only chance of escape.

Chapter two

I turned to face the wall and looked up. Some of the bricks were definitely sticking out. I leapt up and grabbed hold with my fingertips, and then forced my toes into a crack in between two of the courses of bricks. I held on to the jutting-out brick with both hands while I walked up the wall, until I found another foothold. Then I reached up and grabbed at another brick. Once my fingers had a firm grasp of that, I felt the way up the wall with my feet again, pushing at the bricks until I found another crack I could use as a toehold.

"Stop him!" yelled Drutt. "Bring him down!"

There was the sound of running feet on the cobbles, and shouts, and I felt a hand snatch at my ankles. I kicked out and heard a cry of pain. Frantically I reached up, grabbed another jutting brick and hauled myself up higher, and again walked up the wall, pressing my toes into the gaps between the bricks and searching for other bricks to use as a platform to rest my feet.

"Go up after him!" yelled Drutt furiously.

I looked down. I had climbed about ten feet up the wall.

Drutt, Mangle and the boys were standing, glaring up, but none of them was climbing after me.

I looked up. The wall was about twenty feet high. I was halfway to the top. If I could reach that and climb over the wall…

"Go outside and catch him, you idiots!" shouted Drutt.

Immediately some of the boys broke away and ran for the gate to the back lane, and I knew that way of escape had been lost to me. There was now only one way for me to get away and that was to climb to the top of the wall, then make my way along it to the nearest building and climb up to the roof. If I was lucky, I'd be able to get across to the next roof and make my way from roof to roof until I could find a place to scramble down.

I reached up for another handhold on the wall, and as I did there was a crash close to my head and splinters of brick flew painfully into the side of my face. Someone was throwing stones at me.

I looked round and down and saw Mangle stoop and pick up a large, heavy cobble. Then he straightened up, gave an evil, vicious grin and threw the cobble with all his might. I tried to twist to one side, but I felt a crack of searing pain in my head and everything went black…

When I woke up I was lying on a hard cement floor. It was dark, but there was a sliver of daylight filtering through the gaps in the slats of a wooden wall.

I ached. My head hurt from where the cobble had hit me; and so did my legs. I guessed I must have hurt my legs when I fell off the wall.

I knew where I was. I was in a small cupboard off the workhouse laundry room. I had been locked in here often before when I had done something that upset Drutt; right from the time I was very young. In those days I had been frightened of this cupboard: of the dark, the spiders and insects that crawled all over me, of the mice and rats that came out of the holes and cracks in the walls. But that had been when I was small. Now I was nine years old, almost grown, and this cupboard held no fears for me any more; except the fear that I might be shut in and left to starve to death, or be eaten by rats.

My name is Will Reed. I'm an orphan. I never knew who my father was. My mother died here at the workhouse soon after she gave birth to me, so I never knew her either. I've never seen a picture of her, so I don't know what she looked like. They say she died during the great cholera epidemic. People tell me I'm lucky to be alive. Sometimes, I don't feel it.

The proper name of this place is the Plender Street

Infant Pauper Asylum. It's a workhouse for orphans and abandoned children. "Paupers" means we are poor and have no money. Some people say we are fortunate to have a roof over our head and food to eat, but I think it must be one of the worst places in the world. It is like a prison for children. There are about a thousand of us of all ages, from tiny babies to children of 13 who are about to leave. I often say to myself that I only have four more years to suffer this place and then I will be able to go. I don't care that I may not have a roof over my head, I would rather survive on the streets of London than stay and suffer the cruelty of Abel Drutt and Mangle and his bullies.

All of us younger children thought that when Mangle turned 13 he would leave the workhouse and we would be free of him. But instead, Drutt gave him a job as his assistant, and put him in charge of discipline, keeping the children in order. This was a job a bully like Mangle was happy to do. It gave him the chance to carry on being cruel to small children and get away with it.

Sometimes children run away, but they are usually found begging in the streets and brought back. Drutt doesn't like losing any of the children in his care, because he gets paid four shillings and sixpence a week for each child in the workhouse. That money is supposed to be for caring for us, keeping us clean and fed. In fact Drutt keeps the money for himself. We are given a bowl of gruel a day, and scraps of food that Drutt gets from charity: stale bread and biscuits from bakers, mouldy vegetables.

We have mattresses filled with straw laid out on the floors of large rooms, with boys sleeping at one end of the main building and the girls sleeping at the other end. The mattresses stink because many of the children wet themselves at night, and sometimes worse, but they have to stay sleeping on the same stinking mattress until, according to Drutt, they have "learnt their lesson". What that lesson is, I don't know. We are told the lesson is "how to learn to be clean and not soil the bed", but with so many terrified children, that is not a lesson easily learnt, and not in this hard way.

As well as earning money for every child, Drutt makes more cash by hiring children out as workers. Most of the children in the workhouse do things like picking oakum. This means getting old ropes made of hemp, taking them apart bit by bit and putting the short pieces of hemp fibre in sacks. These sacks of hemp are sold to the Navy. I was told they use them to seal the linings of wooden ships and keep them watertight. Picking oakum is horrible, boring work and the hemp pricks at your hands and fingers.

Other people take children out to work. They come and collect the children in the morning and bring them back at the end of the day. That way they don't get the chance to run away.

Some of the children do manage to get away, but they

are never reported as missing to the authorities. That way Drutt keeps getting the money for them, even though they are gone. Luckily for Drutt, with so many children at the workhouse, the few who go missing aren't noticed by the authorities. The people who are supposed to be in charge of the workhouse only come to inspect it about once a year, usually at Christmas, and they would never bother to count the children to make sure every one who is being paid for is there, not with a thousand children in the place. And even if they did, it would be very easy for Drutt and Mangle to make sure that some children were counted twice. After all, to the high-class people who are supposed to be in charge, orphans and foundlings look very much the same as one another: dirty, skinny, and ragged.

I wondered how long I would be kept in the cupboard this time. Once, a long time ago, I tried to run away, and when I'd been brought back I was locked in here for three days. Three days in the dark without food, and just a mug of dirty water to drink, pushed through the partly opened door once a day to make sure I didn't die from thirst. The first two days I didn't drink, worried that I might catch a disease from it. I had been told that the cholera that killed my mother was caught by her drinking dirty water. By the third day I was so thirsty that I drank it, and was promptly sick. I was surprised because, having had nothing to eat, I didn't think there would be anything for me to be sick with. But there was.

I sat in a puddle of stinking vomit in that cupboard for the rest of that day, until Drutt opened the door and let me out. Then he beat me with his cane and told me if I ever ran away again he would beat me until I died.

Is it any wonder I hate this place?

The sound of heavy footsteps on the concrete floor of the laundry room made me go tense. Heavy nail-shod boots. That meant Drutt or Mangle or his bully-boy gang. If it was Mangle then I knew I would be in for a bad time because I had bitten his thumb. And if it was Drutt then I would feel his sharp and cruel cane raising weals and drawing blood on my skin.

I heard the bolt outside the door being slid back, and then daylight flooded into the cupboard, blinding me for a moment.

"Right, Reed!" snarled a nasty voice. "This is where you get it!"

It was Mangle.

Chapter three

"Mr Drutt said we wasn't to hurt him," warned another voice.

I recognized the other voice as belonging to Ketch, one of Mangle's bully cronies.

My eyes had got accustomed to the light now, and I could see Mangle and Ketch standing outside the cupboard.

Mangle spat on the floor and scowled.

"For the moment," he said. "But once Mr Drutt has finished with you, Reed, then it's my turn!" he added nastily.

With that, he and Ketch grabbed me by the arms and dragged me roughly out of the cupboard. I tried to shake free of them, but it was no use. My head and legs still ached, and they were both too strong for me. They half-walked, half-dragged me out of the laundry room and along winding corridors until we were outside Drutt's office. Mangle knocked at the door.

"Come in!" called Drutt.

Mangle opened the door and he and Ketch hauled me into Drutt's room. I was surprised to see another man standing in the office with Drutt. Was this one of the inspectors, I wondered? Had he heard about what had happened and come to check out a complaint against Drutt? Could that be why Drutt had told Mangle and Ketch not to hurt me, when they came for me?

But as I took a closer look at the man, I realized he was definitely not one of the inspectors. When we saw the inspectors, they were nearly always dressed like gentlemen in expensive-looking suits and clean white shirts. This man wore rough-looking clothes, patched in places, and his face and hands were grimy with ingrained dark dust that had worked its way under his skin and become part of his colouring. No, not dust: soot. I guessed he was a chimney sweep.

"We brung Reed for you, Mr Drutt," announced Mangle.

"Good boy," nodded Drutt. "You can go."

Mangle looked at me warily.

"What if he attacks you, Mr Drutt, like he did me?" he asked. "He's mad. He might try and take a bite out of you."

Drutt shook his head.

"Don't worry, Mangle. Even if he gets vicious, I think two fully grown men like myself and Mr Griffin will be able to take care of ourselves." He gave a sly grin. "And there's nowhere in this room he can climb that we can't reach him."

Mangle nodded in agreement, but still looked unhappy about the situation. I could tell he wanted to get his revenge on me for biting his thumb.

"Very well, Mr Drutt," he said. "But me and Ketch will be just outside in case you need us."

With that, Mangle and Ketch left the office and shut the door behind them.

Drutt's office was as shabby as the man himself. Drutt wore the cheapest of clothes. He told the inspectors, and anyone who'd listen, that he couldn't dress in finer clothing because he spent so much money on the children in his care. "The children, my dear sirs," I'd heard him say to someone who came round checking if the workhouse merited charity. "All the money we receive goes to their welfare and upkeep, and I also add what little money of my own I have to ensure they are well fed and kept healthy. People often say to me, Mr Drutt, why do you not dress in fine clothes and have fine furniture, as befits a man in your position, in charge of such a large establishment? But I tell them, sirs, my conscience would not allow it. While there is one child in this great city of ours that is hungry, or needs help, I will spend every penny I have on their well-being rather than on myself. The clothes that I wear, poor but clean, will be my constant reminder of that."

The truth was that Drutt was a miser who hated spending money, and this was a perfect excuse for him. It also made him look like a saint in the eyes of gullible rich people; and so they were happy to give him donations "for the children", all of which he pocketed.

In the same way that he couldn't bear to spend money on his clothes, he didn't spend money on his furnishings

15

but instead scrounged old furniture and carpets and curtains when he could. The piece of patterned rug on the wooden floor was worn so much it was almost threadbare. The office walls had been painted with the cheapest green paint and were flaking. The old wooden desk, burnt and stained in parts, creaked under the weight of the papers that were piled on top of it: files with details of some of the workhouse children.

The only item of furniture that looked in any way comfortable was an old couch, and that was because Drutt would often take a nap on it, rather than go to his own home and spend his own money on coals for his own fire.

The chimney sweep, Mr Griffin, had been standing surveying me quietly all this time, like a man studying a horse before deciding whether to buy it. Suddenly, and in just the same way a man buying a horse does, he bent down and poked at my mouth.

"Open your mouth, boy," he said, and his voice was hoarse and full of phlegm, like a man who coughs a lot. I suppose that came from working with soot and the chimneys.

I opened my mouth, and he examined my teeth, poking at them with one of his stubby soot-stained fingers. Satisfied, he stood up and nodded.

"Good teeth," he grunted.

Drutt gave a low laugh.

"As young Mangle would testify," he chuckled. "Reed nearly

bit through his thumb clear to the bone." He nodded, satisfied. "I can assure you, Mr Griffin, he's healthy enough."

"And agile," put in Griffin. To me he said: "I watched you scale that wall, young fellow. I was seeing Mr Drutt here on a matter of business when there was all that hullabaloo, and next minute there you was a-going up that wall like you was a natural." He nodded again, satisfied. "Griffin, says I to myself, that's the boy for you."

"And he is, I assure you, Mr Griffin," said Drutt; adding in a murmur: "if the price is right, of course."

Griffin shot him a sharp look.

"It will be, you old crook!" he snapped.

Drutt looked shocked. He frowned at Griffin, and cast a wary look at me, then an indignant look back at Griffin.

"Really, Mr Griffin! I must ask you to mind your tongue in front of the boy!"

Griffin looked as if he was going to snap something back at Drutt, but then he obviously changed his mind and just nodded.

"Very well, Mr Drutt," he said. "I'll give him a try tomorrow. See how he shapes up. If he does as well as he looks, we'll fix a price."

Drutt looked doubtfully at Griffin.

"We know the price," he said. "It's the same as the previous one."

"The previous one didn't last, Mr Drutt," said Griffin.

17

"Which meant good time and money spent to no purpose."
He shook his head and looked at me. "You ever been up a
chimney, boy?"

"No," I answered.

"No, *sir*!" barked Drutt sharply, and smacked me round
the back of my head, bringing back the ache. I felt tears of
pain leap into my eyes.

"No, sir," I said.

"That's better," nodded Drutt approvingly. "What time
will you need him for tomorrow, Mr Griffin? I'll see that
he's ready."

"I'll take him now," said Griffin. "I've got a job early in
the morning and I can start getting him shaped up for it
this evening."

"Very well," nodded Drutt. "But if anything happens to
him, you're responsible, and I shall expect recompense. This
boy is worth nearly twelve pounds a year to me."

"Don't worry, he'll be safe. You'll get your money," said
Griffin. To me, he asked: "You got any belongings, boy?"

"No, sir," I said. "Only what I stand up in."

The chimney sweep nodded.

"Then come along with me. We're going to make you a
sweep's boy."

Chapter four

As I walked along the corridor of the workhouse, and then out across the cobbled yard to the main gate, I could feel Mangle's vengeful stare on my back the whole time. He and Ketch glared at me as Griffin and I left Drutt's office, and I could see the disappointment in his face when he realized he wasn't going to get the chance to beat me up today.

We left Plender Street and walked down to Crowndale Road, and then across into Somers Town. Somers Town was only a mile away from the workhouse, but it was a place I did my best to stay away from on the times I went outside. Camden Town's rough, but Somers Town is even rougher. Even the police don't like walking around Somers Town on their own.

We crisscrossed Somers Town through back alleys and narrow lanes, until we came to a ramshackle building with a pair of wooden doors at the front. Griffin unlocked the doors and we went in.

"This is my shop," said Griffin.

Inside it stank of soot. Everything seemed covered with a fine layer of the stuff. Not that there seemed to be much inside: it was an open room, a bit like the laundry room at the workhouse. A few wooden cupboards leant against one wall. A four-wheeled handcart stood in the centre of the floor, with wooden bins on top of the cart.

A set of chimney brushes leaned against a wall. In one corner I saw the glint of glass, and realized that it was a pile of old window frames, most of them broken.

Around the room, leaning against the walls and against one another, were bulging sacks.

"Soot," confirmed Griffin, tapping one of the sacks. "I sells it to the big houses. Their gardeners swear by it for keeping slugs off."

He gestured to a flight of rickety wooden stairs in one corner.

"I live upstairs, over the shop," he said. "You'll go back to the Asylum and stay there generally, but tonight you and I need to have a talk. And away from that perisher Drutt. Come on."

With that Griffin walked over to the stairs and started to go up them. I hesitated. I had heard stories of what some men did to boys when they hired them out from Drutt, and I was wondering if I could run far and get away before Griffin caught me. Griffin became aware that I wasn't behind him, because he stopped and jerked his thumb at me.

"Come on," he said. "I won't hurt you. You're worth money to me."

Then he continued up the stairs. Still wary, I went after him.

The room upstairs also had a thin layer of black soot over everything, but it wasn't as bad as downstairs.

There was a broken-looking bed, a saggy armchair, a dark wooden table with two hard-backed chairs, and a small chest of drawers. A jug stood on the table.

"Thirsty?" he asked.

I nodded.

He took two mugs from the top of the chest of drawers, poured the liquid from the jar into them and handed me one. I smelt it. It was small beer. Everyone drinks small beer instead of water because the water in London is so bad. It stinks and is all sorts of muddy colours. Some say it has so much muck in it, it can almost stand up on its own. People say small beer is better for you because the hops in it kill the germs. Even babies drink small beer once they've finished with their mother's milk.

Griffin motioned for me to sit on one of the wooden chairs and sat down in the armchair. It creaked under his weight as he settled down in it.

"Now, for starters, if anyone asks if you're a chimney sweep's boy, you tell 'em you ain't," he said. "Them interfering busybodies in Parliament have passed an act saying it's against the law for anyone under 21 to go up a chimney." He gave a derisive laugh. "Twenty-one! What idiots! By the time a man gets to that age he's too big to go up a chimney, especially the narrow ones they're building nowadays! See, if they catches us, it's me who has to pay the fine."

"Surely people will know I'm not 21 when we arrive," I said, puzzled.

"Of course they'll know!" agreed Griffin heartily. "Everybody knows. And everybody turns a blind eye to it, except them busybodies in Parliament. If they didn't there wouldn't be one chimney in London that'd be swept. So everyone pretends it don't go on. But it does.

"Next, are you afraid of the dark?"

I thought of the many times I'd spent in that dark cupboard over the years I'd been at the workhouse, and how I'd got used to it.

"No, sir," I said.

"Good," he said. "Because places don't come much blacker than the inside of a chimney." He looked at me thoughtfully. "I know you can climb, so that's no problem. Let's look at your hands and knees."

I looked at him, puzzled.

"My knees?" I echoed.

"Yes," he said. "You'll be using your knees a lot in the chimneys. They're built like they've got stairs made of bricks inside them, but you can't stand up inside a chimney, so you'll be going up those bricks on your knees."

I rolled up my trouser legs and he came over and knelt

down in front of me and examined my knees, first looking at them, and then poking and pinching the skin.

"Now your hands."

He took both my hands in his and examined the palms.

"Your skin's too soft," he said. "We've got to toughen it. Wait there."

He went to the stairs and disappeared down to the room below. I heard something metal being shifted around and liquid being poured. Then Griffin reappeared carrying a bucket. The smell from it was an overpowering smell of fish and salt.

"Brine," he explained, as he put the bucket down. "I gets it from a fishmonger. It's the salt that's left over after they've finished salting the fish. Good stuff. It'll make your skin like leather. You'd better start putting it on tonight."

"Putting it on?"

Griffin nodded.

"It won't help much, but we've got an early start tomorrow so our first chimney is gonna be still warm." He handed me a piece of rag. "Sit down on the floor and soak that rag in the brine and rub it on your knees. Keep doing it. That way your hands will get brine on them as well. The salt will make your skin thicker."

He shrugged. "Some reckon it helps to scrape the skin off your knees first, make 'em bleed, then put the brine on.

Maybe it does, maybe it doesn't. I've tried it both ways and if you ask me, it depends on the boy. Some have got tough skin already and the brine works on its own. Some need a few cuts on their knees for it to work. We'll just have to see what's best for you."

I sat down beside the bucket of stinking fish-smelling water thick with salt and plunged the rag into it.

"How long do I have to do this for?" I asked.

"The more you don't want to burn your hands and knees, then the longer you do it," said Griffin.

He headed back to the stairs.

"I'm going to the pub on the corner, the Red Lion," he said. "If anyone comes asking for me, tell them that's where I am. If I ain't back before you're ready to sleep, just lie down wherever you want, except the bed. That's for me."

With that he went back down the stairs. I heard his feet cross the room below, then the outside door opened, and then banged shut.

I looked around the room for a place where I would sleep. There wasn't anywhere, just bare boards. I'd just have to wrap my coat round me to keep warm tonight while I slept on wooden floorboards. It wouldn't be the first time.

Right now, I'd better get started on making my hands and knees thick if I didn't want to get burnt tomorrow. I took the smelly brine-soaked rag out of the bucket and laid it across my knees, and felt the liquid settle almost like jelly on my skin. I squeezed all the salty liquid out, and then plunged the rag back into the bucket again.

Tomorrow, I would be going up my first chimney.

Chapter five

Next morning we walked from Somers Town north through Camden Town. Griffin pushed his wooden handcart in front of us. It had black sacks and boxes on it to collect the soot, and also some sheets folded up. I carried the set of chimney brushes. There were smaller brushes and scrapers on the handcart.

We arrived at the back of a row of grand-looking houses near Regent's Park and I followed Griffin down the back steps of one of the houses to a cellar area. Griffin knocked at the door and a lady who I guessed was the housekeeper opened it.

"Morning, Mrs Durham," said Griffin. "We've come to sweep the chimney. Everything ready?"

"I've put the sheets down in the rooms to protect the carpet," said Mrs Durham. "The hearth might be a bit warm. The master was up late last night talking. But it can't be helped."

Gesturing at me, Griffin told her: "I've got a new boy starting today. Usual routine?"

"Yes. He knows not to get undressed too soon, doesn't he?"

"No worry, ma'am," smiled Griffin. "He's a good boy. We'll go and get our stuff."

As we walked back up the steps to the handcart, I looked at Griffin.

"Undressed?" I asked him.

"Well you can't go up a chimney with your clothes on," said Griffin. "You'd make a terrible mess when you come down. It stands to reason. You have to take your clothes off before you go up the chimney."

"But say someone sees me?" I said, worried. "One of the maids?"

Griffin shook his head.

"No one will see you. You'll only have your clothes off while you're up the chimney. Soon as you come down it, you put them on again, so you don't make a mess when you walk back through the house. Here, you take the brushes and shovels. I'll carry the sacks and sheets."

We went into the house. Mrs Durham was waiting for us.

"Boots off," she said crisply.

Griffin untied his boots and put them by the back door, and gestured for me to do the same. Once we'd done that we followed Mrs Durham up some stairs and along a corridor to a big room. As we walked I couldn't get over how rich everything was. It was a real posh house. Thick carpets on the floor. Paintings and pictures in frames on the wall. The wood of the banisters shone with polishing.

The first room we went into took my breath away. If the corridor was full of things that showed how rich these people were, the room looked like a treasure house. There were wonderful pieces of china and plates and things on a big dresser, and shelves with books on. The chairs were covered with lovely material. I'd never seen such beautiful things before.

A white sheet had been laid near the big fireplace to protect the carpet, and more sheets had been laid over the furniture near it.

"When you've done this room, the drawing room is next," said Mrs Durham. "I shall be in one of the rooms along the hallway. Call me when you're ready to move on."

"Yes, ma'am," said Griffin.

I followed him over to the fireplace and he knelt down and felt the metal grate.

"Not bad," he said. "It's a bit warm, but not too hot. Nothing you can't cope with." Getting up, he said: "Right. Clothes off."

I hesitated, but then realized there was nothing else I could do. I took my clothes off and stood there naked.

"My, you're a skinny one," said Griffin. "Which is lucky. No use having a chimney boy who gets stuck."

He took the small hand brush and scraper and hung them round my neck by the loops of string tied around their handles.

"You'll need both hands when you go up. You'll find bricks sticking out you can get a grip on with your hands and knees. Climb up, brushing the soot out with the handbrush. If you find a place where the soot has gone hard, use the scraper to get it off. When you've got to the top, remember to keep brushing as you come down, otherwise the chimney will still be dirty."

I knelt down and climbed into the metal grate, and looked up. Above me it was pitch black.

"I can't see the sky at the top," I said.

"That's because the chimney twists and bends as it goes upward," said Griffin. "You won't see the sky until you're near the top."

He began to unfold a dirty sheet.

"I'm going to hang this in front of the fireplace so it stops any soot that comes down from going into the room, so it'll be dark in there. But your eyes will get used to it. If you can't see at first, go by feel."

With that, he draped the sheet over the mouth of the fireplace, and I was plunged into darkness.

I stood with my bare feet on the bars of the metal grate, the brush and scraper dangling from around my neck, and then reached up, feeling for a handhold in the chimney. The bricks were still warm.

Feeling my way up the inside of the chimney in the dark was difficult. The first time I hauled myself up I cracked the top of my head on the bricks, and nearly fell down, but I managed to hang on. I let the pain in my head settle down, and the next time I moved up I went more carefully.

The soot on the first ledge was thick and as I disturbed it, it came up in a cloud, filling my mouth and nostrils and making me cough. I spat out a mouthful of soot and started to brush it off the ledge. I could feel the soot sticking to my skin as it fell past me to the fireplace below.

I climbed up a bit more, feeling for handholds and footholds. I was about to start doing some more brushing, when I thought: "This is silly. If I clean it on the way up, it'll just get filled with soot again from higher up."

The sensible thing would be to get to the top and start brushing and cleaning as I went back down. So that's what I did. I went up, climbing slowly and carefully, from ledge to ledge. The bricks got cooler the higher I went, but the chimney also got narrower. It twisted left and right, and there were a few bends, and in a couple of places there were pieces of slate sticking out that I had to scramble over. I guessed that was to stop rain from coming down the chimney.

In many places the bricks were rough and I grazed the skin of my legs, especially my knees. I was glad I'd coated them with brine the night before.

As I got higher I began to see daylight filtering down from above. At first it was just a glimmer of light, and then it grew brighter, and finally it was a circle of light directly above me.

I pushed my way up until at last I managed to get my head just below where the chimney stack went into the actual chimney pot. I had this fancy of climbing out onto the roof so I could see over the roofs of London, but the chimney pot was just too small for me. Instead I perched on the ledge just below the chimney pot, gripping on tight with my fingers and pressing with my bare feet against the bricks, and smelt the air coming in and listened to the sounds from outside. I swear I even heard a bird singing.

I stayed there for a few minutes, just listening and taking in the sounds and smells of outside. Then I set to work, brushing and scraping the soot and letting it fall down the chimney. As I cleared one ledge of soot and tar I felt my way down to the next foothold, and cleaned around that one. And then down to the next. And so on, until I reached the bottom.

The air at the bottom of the chimney was thick with soot. It was almost impossible to breathe. I did my best to keep my mouth shut, but the soot just dangled in the air and hung around me.

My feet felt the metal bars of the grate through the thick layer of soot that had come down, and I tugged at the sheet hanging over the fireplace.

The sheet twitched, and then was lifted, and Griffin looked in at me.

"Well!" he said, and I could tell from the tone of his voice he was pleased. "You was quick! You sure you went right to the top?"

"Yes, sir," I said. "I saw the sky through the chimney pot."

He looked at the pile of soot filling the grate and spilling out onto the hearth.

"I got to say you've done well," he said. "That's a lot of soot come down. Looks like I won't need to use the big brushes. Good job!"

He held the sheet up so that I could crawl out from the fireplace onto the stone hearth.

"Right," he said. "Help me shovel this stuff into the sacks. Then you can get your clothes back on so we can do the next one."

Chapter six

The chimney in the next room wasn't as hard to do as the first one, because they both ended up at the same chimney pot at the top. I did five fireplaces in that house, and at the end of it I got dressed, and we carried the sacks of soot out to the handcart, and then set off to do another house.

We went to four houses that morning. Then we stopped for a bite of lunch, which was a bit of bread and cheese and half a sausage. After the gruel and scraps of food we got at the workhouse, it was the best meal I'd had in a long time. Then we did some more houses in the afternoon.

Each house followed the same routine: the rooms were protected from falling soot by sheets draped all over. I took my clothes off and climbed up the chimney with the handbrush and scraper. Then we took the soot out to the cart in sacks.

Some chimneys were easier than others. Some were nice and wide. But too wide could be a problem because you might fall. It was best if you could touch all four sides of a chimney to get a good safe grip.

In some houses the fire had only been let go out just before we arrived, and the bricks were so hot I had to wrap cloths round my hands and knees to stop myself being burnt.

But the worst thing was the soot in the air. I could hardly breathe because of it.

The good thing was that Griffin seemed pleased with me, so he was happy to make sure I got good food and proper drink. He even boasted to people he drank with in the pub about how good a climbing boy I was. I know because sometimes he'd take me into the pub with him after we'd finished work for the day and let me have some small beer to drink.

It was after I'd been working for Griffin for about two weeks that we first met Hutch.

Hutch was a tough-looking man who would often be sitting in the pub when Griffin and I arrived. He didn't usually say much, just exchanged pleasantries with the pub landlord, and then sat with his drink, smoking his pipe while he watched and listened to the conversations that went on. On this particular day, Griffin was boasting again about how good a climbing boy I was, and Hutch had moved over to join us at the bar.

"A good climber, you say?" he asked, jerking his thumb at me.

Griffin nodded proudly.

"He's a natural," said Griffin. "You should see him, he goes up a chimney like a monkey up a tree."

Hutch gave a grunt, unimpressed.

"Going up a chimney is one thing," he observed. "But that's inside. Real climbing is when someone can go up in the outside, with the wind pulling at your clothes and when you can see the drop below you."

"He can do that as well!" insisted Griffin. "The first time I saw him he was climbing a wall at the workhouse, and just using his fingers and toes. And he had boots on! Up he went like there was a ladder; but there wasn't."

For the first time Hutch looked at me thoughtfully.

"Is that true?" he asked.

"Yes, sir," I said.

"Up a brick wall?"

"Yes, sir," I said again.

"How did you do it?"

"I looked for the bricks that were sticking out."

"And you weren't scared of falling?"

I remembered that climb only too well. Yes, I may have been scared of falling if I'd thought about it, but I was more scared of what Mangle and Drutt would do to me if they got hold of me.

"No," I said.

Hutch regarded me a little longer, and then he turned to Griffin.

"Mr Griffin," he said, "I think you and I may be able to do a bit of business that might be worthwhile to both of us."

"What sort of business?" asked Griffin suspiciously.

"The sort that has no risk to us but could put a lot of money into our pockets. What do you say?"

Griffin nodded.

"When you put it like that, I'd be a fool to say no."

Hutch looked around carefully at the other people in the pub. Although it was noisy with chatter, he was obviously wary of saying too much in this public place.

"Tell you what," he said. "Let's finish our drinks and go and talk about it at your shop."

"Fair enough," said Griffin. "Come on, boy. Drink up."

We drained our beer glasses and then headed for the street.

As we walked towards Griffin's place my mind was racing. What was the business Hutch was talking about? My guess was it was quite likely something criminal, otherwise Hutch would have talked about it in the pub. I knew it would involve me and the fact that I could climb walls.

I wondered if it was stealing lead from roofs. There's a lot of that goes on in London. Thieves climb up on the roofs of buildings that have a lot of lead flashings, especially large ones like churches, and strip the lead off. Often, the first anyone knows about it is when rain starts to come through the roof where the lead's been removed.

One thing I was sure of: if it was something criminal I

wanted no part of it. I knew that criminals were hanged or sent for transportation to Australia. You used to be hanged for even the smallest thing like stealing a loaf of bread. And it didn't matter what age you were.

My big problem was, how to get out of whatever it was Hutch and Griffin were planning for me? If I ran off, I'd be found for sure and taken back to the workhouse, and Drutt would send me back to Griffin.

I realized that, whatever was going on, I couldn't make any move until I found out what it was Hutch and Griffin had in mind for me.

Chapter seven

"Burglary?" Griffin said, and looked at Hutch wide-eyed.

Hutch nodded.

We were back in Griffin's place. Griffin and Hutch were sitting at the table and I was on the floor.

I let the word settle in my mind. Burglary! Definitely a criminal offence.

"It'll be easy," said Hutch. "We'll only be going into houses that are empty."

"How do you know they'll be empty?" asked Griffin.

"Local knowledge," replied Hutch. He winked. "Chimney sweeps, for one thing. People often have their chimney swept when they are going away for a few days. They also know the layout of the inside of the house.

"Then there's other tradespeople. Plumbers, carpenters, joiners, grocers and the like.

"Plus there are servants who talk. Chatter over a drink in a pub. Happy to boast how wealthy their master is, and how their mistress has got this and that jewellery stashed in her bedside table. And, most important, when they're off to some grand do at the theatre, or away for a few days in their country place."

He chuckled.

"All that boasting and idle chatter. All you have to do is listen and you know who's got what and when they won't be at home. It's easy pickings!"

Griffin nodded, but he looked uncertain.

"Where's the boy come in?" he asked, gesturing at me.

"Because it's too dangerous trying to break in downstairs. You try and jemmy a door or a window and someone's bound to see you and raise the alarm. No, the safest way is up on the roof and through a skylight. And the best people for doing that are climbing boys. Chimney boys, like your monkey here.

"In through the skylight, then down the stairs and open the back door, where yours truly will be waiting, standing there like any respectable person. In I go, and then me and the boy do the business. Jewellery. Cash. All items not too easily traced. Nothing too bulky and hard to carry.

"We've got plenty of time to do it because no one else is in the house. We'll know that because I'll have checked it out first, made sure the people are away. Checked out where the safe is. Where the mistress keeps her valuables."

Griffin sat in silence, thinking it over.

"I still say it's risky," he said. "Say you're caught?"

"How can we be caught?" said Hutch. "Like I said, no one's

in the house. We do it at night so we're not seen. There's no noise of us getting in, so no alarm being raised."

"Say the skylight's shut?" I said.

Hutch looked at me and laughed.

"The monkey's awake!" he chuckled.

"If the skylight's shut and locked, I'd have to break it to get in. That would make a noise and someone would raise the alarm."

"He's got a point," agreed Griffin, nodding.

I was relieved to hear him say that. I wanted nothing to do with this and the sooner they stopped talking about it, the better. But Hutch just gave another little chuckle.

"A locked skylight is no problem," he said. "As we came in I saw you got some old window frames in your yard."

Griffin nodded.

"I takes 'em away sometimes for people when they have new windows put in. Things like that are always handy."

"Can you spare one?" asked Hutch. He felt inside his pocket and produced a couple of coins. "I'll pay you for it."

Griffin took the money and nodded.

"Right," said Hutch. "Let's go downstairs and we'll show the monkey how to do the business."

I didn't like being referred to as "the monkey", but I thought it best to say as little as possible. Once I found out everything, then I could say what I felt.

We went downstairs to the open area, and Hutch selected

40

one of the smaller window frames that Griffin had stacked together in the corner. This window frame was complete with the outer frame and catches, as if it had come straight out of the wall where it had once been.

Hutch laid the whole frame on the bench.

"Right, now, monkey—" he began.

"My name's Will," I corrected him. This "monkey" business was starting to annoy me.

Hutch shot me a look, and then laughed.

"Sensitive, ain't you, young 'un," he said. "All right, *Will*, come here and pay attention."

I joined him and Griffin at the bench and stood looking at the window frame. Hutch pointed to the place where the window catch held the opening part of the window to the outer frame.

"See that?" he said. "That's the catch and it's shut. The only way to get hold of it is by breaking the glass and reaching in."

"That's what I said before," I told him.

Hutch grinned. He opened his bag and took out a square of hessian sacking and a tin of something. He unscrewed the top of the tin. He gave it to me to smell.

"Tar," I said.

"Correct," he said.

He poured some of the thick, black, oozing liquid onto the pane of glass at the edge of the window, near to where the window catch was. Then he pushed the square of hessian sacking onto the black tar.

"Give that a few seconds for it to soak in and grip," he said.

Hutch reached into his pocket and pulled out what looked like a small penknife. Only, instead of a blade it had what looked like a small wheel at the end. He held it up proudly.

"This is a glass cutter," he said. "Watch."

He gave a tug at the piece of sacking he'd stuck to the window. It held firm. Then, holding on to the sacking with one hand, he began to cut a groove in the glass around the piece of sacking with the glass cutter.

"Don't make the hole too big," he said. "Otherwise the weight of the glass can make it fall off the sacking. You only need it big enough to be able to get your hand in so you can open the window catch."

He finished cutting the groove in the glass and dropped the glass cutter back into his pocket. I noticed he still had hold of the sacking stuck to the window.

From his pocket he took another tool: a short stick with a wide soft pad at one end.

"Now, you bang the glass where you've cut it. Not too light or it won't separate the glass along the cut. You got to get it just right. Like this."

Hutch jabbed the padded end of the stick onto the glass at the place he'd cut it. There was the barest "crack", and the cut section of glass moved down making a hole.

"Not too hard either, because you can lose it if it falls right through into the house. But if that happens it's not too bad. Depends how far it's got to fall. But the best and quietest way is to pull it back out … like so."

And Hutch gently pulled at the sacking, and a square of glass came up with it, leaving a clear hole near the catch.

Hutch laid the section of tarred glass down on the bench, then reached through the hole and undid the window catch.

"See?" he said smugly. "Easy."

I felt a shudder go through me. Watching Hutch do it, it did look easy. Desperately I tried to think of a way out of this. And then the realization came to me.

"It won't work," I said. "I'm only allowed out in the daytime. I have to go back to the workhouse at night. If I'm not there then Mr Drutt can't count me as being there, and he won't get paid for me. Mr Drutt won't let me stay out at night."

Griffin and Hutch looked at each other thoughtfully.

"He's got a point," said Griffin. "Drutt does love his money. He gets four and sixpence a week for each child. Say there's an inspection one night with them counting the children at the workhouse?"

There'd never been an inspection at the workhouse as far as I knew it, only the one at Christmas. But I kept quiet about that. I wanted them to be worried enough not to use me for burgling.

Hutch thought about it and nodded.

"It is a good point," he said. "Is this boy as good a climber as you say he is?"

"Better," said Griffin enthusiastically. "Like I said, he can go up a wall like a monkey up a tree."

"Then it might be worth talking to Mr Drutt about cutting him in," said Hutch. "After all, there's money to be made here, and it'd be a pity to lose it just for the sake of a few shillings."

Chapter eight

I walked back to the workhouse with Griffin and Hutch. They seemed very casual and relaxed about the whole burglary thing, chatting and laughing as we walked. Me, I felt sick. My stomach felt like it was being tied in a knot.

It was all right for Griffin. He wouldn't be involved in carrying out the burglaries. He'd just be getting money from Hutch for "borrowing" me. And Hutch would be outside the house, waiting for me to open the door and let him in. If anything went wrong and the alarm was raised, all Hutch had to do was walk away. I was the one who'd be caught. I would be the one with the burglar's tools: the piece of sack, the tin of tar, and the glass cutter. There had to be a way out of this for me! But how? My one hope now was that Drutt would be afraid to get involved in case things went wrong and he got arrested. Beneath his bullying ways, Drutt was a coward. But if Hutch offered him enough money, would that overcome Drutt's cowardice?

We got to the workhouse and walked along the corridor to Drutt's office. Griffin knocked at the door, and I heard Drutt call: "Come in!"

Hutch put his hand on my shoulder.

"You stay here for the moment," he said. "Let me and Mr Griffin have our talk with Mr Drutt first."

The pair of them went into the office and left me standing outside. I leant against the door and did my best to hear what they were saying, but the door was made of thick wood and all I could hear were their voices. They were talking conversationally, no raised voices or sudden shouts. I pressed my ear against the door even harder to try and hear what was going on. I was so intent on this that I didn't hear the footsteps creeping up behind me. Suddenly I felt a hand grab my ear and pull it painfully.

"Listening at doors, eh!" snarled a voice nastily.

It was Mangle.

Behind him stood Ketch, and another of Mangle's gang of bullies, a boy called Dobson.

"We'll show you what happens to people who listen at doors!" spat Mangle.

He grabbed me and swung me round towards Ketch and Dobson, who caught me by the arms and held me. They both had broad grins on their faces.

"What you need is a good kicking!" smirked Mangle.

And as Ketch and Dobson held me like a target, Mangle aimed a kick at my groin. I just managed to sway to one side, but as it was Mangle's boot caught on my thigh and the pain shot through me. I struggled to break free from the hold Ketch and Dobson had on me, but they were too strong.

Mangle grinned and positioned himself to aim another kick at me, but this time I managed to get one in first, my boot coming up and cracking him on his knee.

Mangle gave a howl of pain and began hopping about on one leg, clutching his injured knee. I struggled against Ketch and Dobson, but they just increased their grip and held me even tighter.

Mangle stopped hopping around and the look he gave me was one of pure venom.

"I'm gonna cripple you for that, you worm!" he raged.

As he swung his foot back, the office door opened and Drutt stood in the doorway, glaring out.

"What on earth is all this row going on?!" he demanded.

Mangle put his foot down.

"We caught him listening at your door, Mr Drutt," he explained. "We was punishing him for it."

Drutt looked at me, still being held tightly and painfully by Ketch and Dobson. Griffin and Hutch had appeared behind Drutt now and were looking over his shoulder at the scene. Drutt looked like a man in a spot, caught being asked to choose between two different opinions, and not wanting to choose either. On one hand he had to let Mangle know he would back him at all times, no matter how cruel Mangle was. That was how Drutt kept discipline in this place. But on the other hand, Griffin and Hutch were dangling money in front of him.

Money won.

"Let Reed go at once!" snapped Drutt.

Mangle, Ketch and Dobson gaped at Drutt in astonishment.

"But Mr Drutt…" protested Mangle.

"I said let Reed go!" repeated Drutt, his voice even firmer this time.

Ketch and Dobson released my arms.

"These gentlemen have expressed an interest in Reed," continued Drutt in a pompous tone. "It would be best if he was not harmed. Is that clear, Mangle?"

Mangle said nothing, but his face was contorted with a mixture of anger and bewilderment. He scowled.

"I said: is that clear, Mangle?" demanded Drutt.

Mangle breathed angrily and hard for a few seconds, and then said, "Yes, Mr Drutt," in a harsh voice, as if his answer was being forced out of him between clenched teeth.

"Good," said Drutt. "You may go about your business, now." To me he said: "Reed, you will stay here and wait until I have finished my discussion with these two gentlemen."

With that, Drutt, Griffin and Hutch went back inside the office and shut the door.

Mangle, Ketch and Dobson looked at me. Mangle, particularly, looked as if he would burst with his pent-up anger. He came up to me and thrust his face close to mine. I could smell the violence and rage coming off him.

"This ain't over," he threatened me menacingly. "One day those *gentlemen* …" and at that word he turned and spat on the floor, "won't be around. And when that happens, you're mine. And first I'm gonna cripple you, and then I'm gonna kill you."

He turned to Ketch and Dobson.

"Come on. Let's leave this worm. He ain't worth it."

With that, the three of them walked off.

I took my place again outside the door of the office. It would be a waste of time listening at the door now. Drutt's attitude had said it all. He had agreed. I was going to be a burglar.

Chapter nine

I stood outside the office for another quarter of an hour before the door opened again. Drutt didn't even look at me this time. He shook hands with both Griffin and Hutch as they left, and then shut the door.

"Right," said Griffin. "I've got to get back to my shop. Mr Hutch here wants a little word with you in private, Will. I'll pick you up as usual tomorrow morning."

With that, Griffin walked off.

Hutch looked down at me and put his hand on my shoulder.

"No one likes being around when the difficult things have to be said," he grinned. But it was a grin without any humour in it. I looked into his eyes, and in them I saw for the first time that Hutch was a very dangerous man indeed. "Come on, monkey. You and I need to have a little talk."

He steered me firmly along the corridor and out into the workhouse yard. As always, the older children were sitting around in groups, talking, while the younger ones ran around or played games with pebbles and rags.

"Let's find ourselves somewhere out of earshot," said

Hutch, and he steered me to a corner of the yard which was empty of anyone but us. He sat down on an old box and patted it for me to sit beside him.

"Right, Will," he said. "If we're going to be working together, we need to get a few things straight."

I wanted to burst out and say, "I'm not going to be working with you! I won't be a burglar!" But the hard look in his eyes sent a chill down my spine. For the moment I decided just to shut up and listen. I'd find a way out of this later.

"First, what you're doing working as a chimney boy for a sweep is against the law," said Hutch. "You know that, right?"

I nodded.

"But if you're caught the worst that happens is you have to stop work and Griffin gets a fine. But what we're talking about with *our* work is different. If we get caught…" Here, he ran his hand across his throat. Then he smiled that same awful smile as before. "So, I don't get caught. Now they may catch *you*. They shouldn't, but these things happen. And I can see you're a bright enough boy to understand that. Yes?"

Again, I said nothing, just nodded. I'd understood that right from the start.

"Good," said Hutch. "Then it's important that you know that if you get caught and you mention my name, or give a description of me to the police, bad things will happen to you. Very bad things. You understand?"

"Yes, sir," I said.

"Good," he nodded. He smiled again, that dreadful threatening smile. "Now it could be that you're thinking: I've got to get out of this. I'll run away and no one will find me."

"No, sir!" I protested quickly. Too quickly.

This time Hutch shook his head.

"Wrong answer," he said with a sad sigh. "You and I both know that's what you're thinking. Well you'd better know that I'm not going to let that happen. I've invested too much time and money in you to let you slip through my fingers. If you run off from here, or while you're out with me, or with Griffin, I shall track you down. Trust me, Will, I have friends everywhere. I need them in my business so I know what's going on. And those friends will find you for me. Am I making myself clear?"

I gulped, and nodded.

"Yes, sir," I said. And now I felt an icy hand clutching at my chest. I was trapped. I knew it, and Hutch knew it.

"Good," said Hutch. "It's important we understand one another. Now, for payment, you'll get a share of whatever we take. It won't be a big share because there's a lot of people to pay out. I've got to pay Griffin for the lending of you. I've got to pay Drutt to keep his mouth shut. There's fences to pay for getting rid of jewellery and such-like." Fences are what they call people who sell stolen goods. "There's a lot of expenses in this game, Will. But you'll get your share. Certainly more than you get for being a chimney sweep's boy.

"Which brings me to another point. I've arranged with Griffin that you won't be going up any chimneys in the afternoon. I need you clean for our work. If you go in smelling of soot and leaving sooty prints all over the place, it'll give our game away. So I've told Griffin that when I come and collect you I want you washed and scrubbed clean. And you'll wear a different set of clothes when we go out. Ones without any soot on."

I looked at him, shocked. Washed, scrubbed and clean? We never washed at the workhouse. Not all over, anyway. Now and then our face and hands. Except at Christmas when we knew the rich people were coming and Drutt said we mustn't smell bad. Too much washing was bad for you. It made you get sickly. Everyone knew that.

"What's the matter?" he asked, seeing the expression on my face.

"If you wash too much it's bad for you," I said.

Hutch smiled.

"Not in my book," he said. "For one thing, it's not as bad as leaving soot all over the place when we go in. Trust me. I know what I'm doing, Will."

He gave me a grin.

"Now, get a good night's sleep. Tomorrow, we go to work."

Chapter ten

The next day, after Griffin and I had done the chimneys, we went back to Griffin's shop and I took my clothes off and he stood me in a tin bath under a tap and ran cold water on me, while I scrubbed myself. It was horrible. The water was cold, and when the layers of dirt came off me and ran into the bath I started to shiver. I was sure I was going to get ill because of it.

By the time Hutch came to collect me when it was dark, I was dressed in clean clothes. Hutch carried a bag with his burgling tools in, and some sacks folded up under his arm.

"Right, monkey," he said. "Let's go." To Griffin he added: "I'll take him back to the workhouse afterwards. You can collect him from there tomorrow morning."

"What about my money?" asked Griffin.

"Don't worry, you'll get your share," said Hutch.

I followed Hutch out of Griffin's shop and we headed out of Somers Town northwards. I noticed that Hutch kept to the back alleys, even though it was dark, so we wouldn't be easily spotted.

We got to the house that Hutch had made his target, and

I recognized it at once. It was the same house where I had cleaned my very first chimneys. Hutch must have felt my shock, because he let out a small, dry laugh.

"You recognize it, eh, monkey?" he chuckled. "Yes, it's the same house where you started climbing chimneys. I thought it might make it easier for you, seeing as you've been inside it once already. You'll know your way around, so to speak. Everyone's out tonight so it'll be dead safe.

"Remember, most important: once you're inside, no lights. Don't want to make the neighbours suspicious, especially if they know the family are away. Get inside, down the stairs, and open the back door for me. And be quick. Right?"

"Yes, sir," I said.

He hung the bag with the tar, sacking, glass cutter and padded stick around my neck.

"That there," he said, pointing to a drainpipe fixed to the wall that led up to the guttering on the edge of the roof. "Think you can climb it?"

"If it's strong," I said.

"It's strong," he said. "It shouldn't come away from the wall. I checked it." He took a last look round to make sure no one was watching, and then nudged me towards the drainpipe. "Right, up you go. And no noise."

I grabbed hold of the drainpipe and gave it a tug. It felt firm enough. Using it as my handhold, I began to climb, pressing my boots against the wall and pulling myself upwards hand over hand. All the time I was climbing I expected someone to call out "Stop thief!", or a police whistle to blow. Nothing. The night was quiet. Hutch had chosen the time well. I guessed he knew what time the police patrols walked these streets, and in which houses people stayed up late so they might look out of their windows.

Up, up I went. Higher and higher. It was easier than when I'd climbed the wall at the workhouse. It was easier than climbing up the inside of a chimney because it was straight rather than twisting and turning, and cramped and narrow. But in another way, it was harder, because I could feel the wind tugging at me as I got higher, and I knew that if I fell from this height I wouldn't be able to grab hold of bricks inside the chimney. If I fell here, I'd die.

I reached the iron guttering and grabbed hold of it, and felt it give. For a moment I thought it was going to come away from the edge of the roof. I steadied myself, then took a chance, hauling myself up so my knees were on the gutter and I was able to get a hold on the roof slates.

I balanced myself on the roof on my hands and knees, and worked my way up towards the skylight. The roof slates felt a bit slippery beneath me. I was glad it hadn't been raining otherwise I would have slid down them and gone straight off the edge of the roof.

When I reached the skylight I used the brick-and-wood frame around it as a handhold to help me stand up.

So far, so good. I wanted to stop and take a good look around from the roof, gaze at London as far as the eye could see from up here, but the knot of fear in my stomach at the thought of getting caught drove me on. I did the trick with the tar and the piece of sacking on the glass by the window catch, as Hutch had shown me. As I banged the section of cut glass with the end of the padded stick, I expected it to shatter with a dreadful noise which would bring people running, but it worked exactly as Hutch had said it would.

I pulled the piece of glass out, undid the window catch and lifted the skylight open.

That done, I balanced myself on the edge of the skylight, holding on tightly with my hands, and then let myself drop down, so I was hanging from the edge of the skylight.

Because it was dark inside the house I couldn't tell how far the drop to the floor below me was. At least I knew that it didn't drop onto a flight of stairs, which had been my main fear.

I hung for a second, and then let myself fall. I hit the floor and rolled so I wouldn't hurt myself, taking care to hold on to the tin of tar inside the bag so it didn't burst open.

I got up and stood, letting my eyes get used to the darkness inside the house. Gradually I began to see shapes in the moonlight coming in from the skylight. I recognized this landing from when I'd come to the house to do the chimneys. This top floor was where the children's playroom was. On the next floor down were the main bedrooms. Then down to the ground floor where the drawing room was. And below that were the kitchen and the place where the servants lived and worked.

I set off along the landing, and then down the stairs, moving as quick as I could in the darkness, but taking care not to go too fast in case I tripped and fell.

I got to the back door next to the kitchen, pulled the bolts back and opened it. Hutch was there waiting. He slid in, shut the door and bolted it again.

"Good boy," he said. "Right, let's see what they've got on offer for us. We'll start with the bedrooms."

Up the stairs we went to the main bedrooms. Hutch seemed to know exactly what he was looking for. He opened drawers and cabinets, taking mainly small items which he put in one of the sacks. When he found cash, he stuffed it into his pockets. I guessed all the information he picked up – where people kept their jewellery, their money and other valuables – meant he could move so much more quickly and not waste time.

After we'd done the bedrooms I followed him downstairs. Once again, it was small items he was after, but they all looked valuable. Jewellery, precious stones, gold and silver. I expect these small items were easier to sell on than big ones would be.

Finally, it was into the kitchen, where he started taking the good silver cutlery from the big dresser. By now Hutch's sack was full. He dumped the rest of the loot into my sack.

"Right," he said. "That's a good haul. Time to go."

He unbolted the door and we slipped out into the cellar area, and then up the stairs to the street. Soon we were on our way, using the back alleys and lanes, me carrying one sack and Hutch the other. The whole time we were on the move my heart was in my mouth in case we were stopped by a policeman, but we weren't.

We arrived at the workhouse and he knocked at the main door. It opened, as if it had been arranged, by one of the old women who were the night doorkeepers. Hutch slipped her a coin, and then took the sack from me.

"Good boy, monkey," he said. "Well done. I'll see you tomorrow night."

With that, he disappeared, hurrying off, bowed down under the weight of both sacks. I went in, and headed for my bed.

Chapter eleven

And so I became a burglar.

I knew it was against the law and wrong, and I didn't want to be a criminal. But what choice did I have?

Perhaps I could have gone to the police and told them, but would they protect me against Hutch's friends? The ones he said would torture and kill me. And if I told the whole story, that would bring in Drutt. And Drutt would deny everything. Not only that, to protect himself from Hutch he would tell the police that I was a liar. Who would the authorities believe? Me, an orphan, or the Master of one of London's biggest workhouses for children? A man who made great claims to spend all his own money doing charitable works for children.

No, it was no use. I was trapped into being a criminal. And I was not alone. London is a nest of thieves and crooks, and many of them use children. Robbers and burglars use children as look-outs when carrying out a job. Pickpockets use children to help them distract their victims. Many crooks train children as pickpockets because the children's small fingers can dip into a pocket with much more ease than an adult's larger hand.

The one thing we all had in common was that none of us could escape our criminal masters. They were bigger and more powerful than us children. They all knew one another, and it was in their best interests to make sure that any children they employed stayed tied to them. So they watched out for each other. If a child tried to leave a gang, then they made sure that child was brought back in line, often on pain of death.

Over the next two weeks my routine was the same. I would be collected from the workhouse by Griffin and taken to clean chimneys during the day. Maybe we'd do two or three chimneys. Then, at the end of the day, Griffin would take me back to his place and get me ready for Hutch to take me burgling.

By the end of the second week there was still no sign of Hutch paying me my share he'd promised me, and I asked him about it.

"Don't trust me, eh?" he said.

The truth was, I didn't trust him. I was taking the risk as well as him. More so, if you thought that it was me who did the actual climbing and breaking in. And so far I had nothing to show for it.

"Don't worry," he assured me. "I'll settle up with you next week."

It was at the start of the next week when Griffin sounded

61

a warning. It happened one night when Hutch came to Griffin's place to collect me. I was washed, scrubbed and wearing my clean clothes, ready to go, when Hutch arrived.

"Ready, monkey?" he asked.

I got up, but Griffin put a hand on my shoulder to stop me.

"I think you ought to give it a rest," he said.

I'd noticed he had looked worried during the day.

"Why?" asked Hutch.

"The word on the street is that there've been too many burglaries of late. People are getting upset. The police have been told to be extra watchful."

"So?" shrugged Hutch. "They can be watchful, but it doesn't mean we're going to be caught. I've told you, I always make sure my information is safe and sure. Empty houses only."

Griffin shook his head.

"It's getting too risky," he advised. "They say they're putting police inside some of the houses that people think are empty."

Hutch laughed.

"Scare stories," he said. "Trust me, I know which houses are safe to do and which aren't."

"Yes, but say they're watching the house next to the one you're doing?" persisted Griffin. "They might see Will going up the pipe to the roof." He chewed his lip, nervously. "It's not just you who's at risk, you know. If you get caught they'll come to me as well. I'll be for the chop."

Hutch smiled and patted Griffin reassuringly on the shoulder.

"You're worrying unnecessarily," he said. Then he added with a sigh: "But, just in case, I will take a break." Griffin stopped chewing his lip and looked pleased, a look that vanished as Hutch added: "From tomorrow, for a few days."

"Tomorrow could be too late," urged Griffin. "You oughtn't to go out tonight."

I stood there, waiting, my heart in my mouth, willing Hutch to agree with Griffin and decide not to go. But Hutch shook his head.

"I've got responsibilities," he said. "Tonight's job is a special. There's someone willing to pay big money for a certain something that's in the house. And the family are only going to be away tonight. So it's got to be done tonight. But don't worry. After this one, like I said, we'll take a few days' rest until things quieten down."

Turning to me, he said: "Come on, Will, my little monkey. Let's go to work."

Chapter twelve

That night as Hutch and I set off from Griffin's shop, we were both more tense than usual. I was frightened because of what Griffin had said. I was terrified that the police might be lying in wait for us inside the house, or anywhere along the way. Hutch was tense too, but he blamed it on me, accusing me of making him feel uncomfortable with my nervousness.

He'd chosen another of the houses I'd been to with Griffin to clean their chimneys. My guess was that he was hoping this might speed things up for me once I was inside. This time when we reached the back of the house he didn't come with me into the cellar area.

"I'll stay back here in the shadows and watch out for you," he said. "I'll come when you open the back door."

"I don't like it," I said. "Say the police are inside the house, waiting?"

"They won't be," he snapped. "My information is always good. The house is empty. Now hurry up and get up that drainpipe."

He moved back into the shadow of an alley, and I headed for the cellar of the house, my bag banging against my side.

I went down the steps to the cellar area, then stopped and looked around. I couldn't see anyone about. So far, so good. But there was still something that didn't feel right.

I stood there, listening, trying to see what was making me nervous. But everything looked normal. It must just have been Griffin talking about police traps that had set my nerves on edge. Oh well, the sooner I did this, the sooner it would be over. And Hutch had promised it would be the last for a while.

I went to the drainpipe, took a handhold on it and began to climb. Up I went, hands holding the drainpipe, feet pressed against the brick wall. I was about fifteen feet off the ground when I heard the sound of a police whistle, followed by another a bit further away. Then there was the crashing of heavy boots heading towards the house.

I didn't even look round to see where they were coming from. I began to slide down the drainpipe as fast as I could, set on running off as soon as my feet touched the ground. But I was too late. Even before I reached the ground two policemen were on me. One pulled me away from the drainpipe and threw me to the ground, and the other fell on me, crushing me. All the while the police whistles kept blowing and there were shouts of "Got him!" Then more policemen appeared, running, truncheons drawn, and I knew I was caught.

They took me to a police station where I was put into a room with a detective. Three uniformed policemen stood around in the room with us, looking as if they were ready to jump on me if I tried anything.

The detective pointed at a chair next to a table, and I sat down. On the table was my bag with my burglar tools: the tar, the sacking, the glass cutter and the stick.

"So you're our burglar," said the detective.

I said nothing.

"You might as well admit it," continued the detective. "After all, we caught you with your tools." And he tapped the bag.

Still I said nothing.

"You know burglary's a hanging offence?" he asked.

This time I said, "No." I was hoping there might be a way out of this.

"Ah, you do talk then," said the detective. "You can start by giving us your name."

I shut my mouth firmly.

The detective gave a sigh.

"Look, we can do this the easy way or we can do it the hard way," he said. "If we do it the easy way that might put me in a good mood and I might be able to help you. Maybe you won't hang. But if you make me do it the hard way, you're going to annoy me, and then I'll make sure they throw the book at you. Hanging, definitely. And maybe a flogging before they hang you. So, what's it to be?"

I thought of the threat Hutch had made to me if I talked. I knew he meant it.

The detective scowled.

"You're starting to annoy me," he said. "By the look of you I'm guessing you're a workhouse boy, so it won't take us long to find out where you're from and who you are. You could save us a lot of bother by just telling us your name."

I thought it over. Telling him my name should be all right. All right, they might track me back to the Plender Street Asylum, but that's as far as it would go. Drutt would deny any knowledge of me, maybe even claim I had run away.

"My name's William Reed," I told him.

The detective smiled.

"Good boy," he said. "That's a start. Now, who are you working for?"

Once again, I said nothing. The detective sighed, wearily.

"Look, you don't expect me to believe you did these burglaries all on your own, do you? For one thing, the stuff that was taken would be too heavy for you to carry. Next, the thief knew exactly what he was looking for each time. That makes him a professional. If you give me his name, I'll see the judge goes easy on you. Maybe just get you transported or something. Start a whole new life in the colonies. That's better than hanging, surely?"

I kept my mouth firmly shut. For one thing, I didn't believe him about getting me a lighter sentence. And, for another, even if I did, I knew what Hutch was capable of, and I knew he'd carry out his threat to kill me.

The detective sat looking at me for a bit, then he scowled.

"I haven't got time to waste on this," he said. "I think maybe a few days in Newgate Prison might bring you to your senses." He stood up and turned to the policemen. "Put him in the next van and send him to Newgate. He can stay there till his trial."

To me, he added: "It's your choice. Tell me the name of the man you're working for and I'll help you. Keep silent like this, and I'll make sure you hang. It's your choice."

Chapter thirteen

There were twelve of us inside the back of the police van, six on a bench at each side.. We were chained together, six on a chain. Manacles were on our wrists and each chain ran through the manacles to a padlock which was fixed to a metal bolt in the back wall of the van. Two police constables sat on a bench at the back, next to the locks. They carried hard wooden truncheons, ready to hit us if any of us caused trouble.

None of us looked like we were going to be starting any trouble. Most of us sat with our heads down in misery, and listened to the sound of the horses' hooves as they clip-clopped over the road, taking us to Newgate Prison. One man sat bolt upright, his face looking grimly defiant. I noticed the constables kept a special watch on him, as if he was the one most likely to cause trouble.

I was the youngest in the van. Next to me was a big brute of a man with gashes on his forehead and dried blood on his face. Opposite me were two women, one of whom was crying. The other woman tried to put her arms round her to comfort her, but it was impossible for her with the manacles and chains on her wrists.

Newgate Prison. All of us knew about it, even if not all of

us had seen it. It was the most terrifying prison in England. Up till two years before, 1868, they held public hangings at the gallows just outside the prison gate in Newgate Street. Thousands of people would come to see the hangings. Then they decided to stop hanging people in public and the gallows was moved inside the prison. A lot of people complained about that, because going to see a hanging was one of the best entertainments for ordinary people, and especially because it was free.

The van rocked from side to side as we journeyed through the streets. I couldn't see where we were because the back of the van didn't have any windows in it, but I reckoned we must be almost there because of the time we'd been travelling. Then we heard the driver outside call "Whoa!" to the horses, and the sound of their hooves slowed down and then stopped.

We heard the sound of heavy metal gates being opened, and voices calling out instructions and giving directions, though I couldn't make out what was being said. The van gave a jerk and moved forward again.

The sound beneath the iron wheels of the police van was different; there was more of an echo to it.

Then I heard the doors give a metal clang as they were shut behind us and the sound of bolts being slid shut.

We were in Newgate Prison.

Chapter fourteen

I was pushed into a cell with two bunks in it. One of the bunks had a thin grimy mattress. The other was stripped bare, just a wooden board fixed to the wall.

"There's usually two in a cell, but you're lucky," said the warder who'd brought me from the police van to the cell. "The bloke who was going to be in here with you died yesterday. Killed himself. Slashed his wrists with a bit of broken metal." He shook his head. "All that blood ruined a good mattress. Still, you shouldn't be alone for long. There's always new people coming in to this place, and not many going out."

He stepped out of the cell and nodded to the turnkey, who slammed the door shut and locked it. The sound of that heavy metal door shutting and the lock being turned so firmly sounded as if part of my soul was being locked out of me.

I looked round the cell. There wasn't much to look at. There were the two bunks and a bucket in one corner for use as a toilet.

There was one tiny window set high up in the wall, too high

for anyone to reach. Thick iron bars were set close together across the window.

I examined the door of the cell. It was made of thick studded iron. High up, at about the level of an adult's eyes, there was a spy-hole with a piece of metal covering it from the outside.

Even though the door and the wall were thick, I could hear some sounds outside my cell: the sound of metal-nailed boots marching on the flagstones of the corridor. Keys being rattled. The banging of hard wood against metal and stone as the officers rattled their truncheons along the walls of the corridor and against the cell doors. Now and then in the distance I thought I could hear a cry of misery, but that could have been my imagination.

I sat down on the bunk and looked at the cell, and listened to the sounds outside. Dust hung in the air, swirling round in the narrow shaft of light that came into the cell from the tiny barred window. I sat and looked at the dust, and the stones in the wall of the cell, and the wooden boards of the bunk opposite me. There were still bloodstains on the wooden boards of the bunk where the man who'd killed himself the day before had bled to death. I wondered why he'd killed himself? Guilt? Fear? Had the misery of this place finally snapped his mind? I sat on the bunk and looked at the cell, and listened to the sounds. There was nothing else I could do. I was in hell.

"Visitor for William Reed!"

I was startled to hear my name being called out from the corridor. Who would be visiting me? Surely it wouldn't be Hutch or Griffin. They'd make sure they stayed well away from me.

"William Reed!" I heard the turnkey call out again.

"Here!" I shouted.

The metal shutter over the spy-hole in my cell door was lifted and an eye looked in at me. Then there was the sound of a key turning in the lock and the cell door opened. The turnkey motioned for me to step out. A prison warder was standing behind him.

"This is prisoner Reed," the turnkey announced to the warder, who nodded and prodded me with the end of his wooden truncheon.

"The visiting room's at the end of the corridor," he said. "If you try anything, you'll feel the weight of this." And he prodded me with the truncheon again. "Trust me, I can break a bone with this. Understood?"

I nodded and set off in the direction he showed me, along the corridor. The warder walked beside me, the metal studs on the soles of his boots ringing on the flagstone paving of the corridor. From inside some of the cells we passed came the sound of loud wailing, and even screaming, but the warder showed no emotion.

We reached a wooden door and the warder knocked at it.

There was the sound of a key being turned, then the door swung open and I was in the visiting room.

Row upon row of tables were crammed close together, with two chairs at each.

Grim-faced warders patrolled the spaces between the tables, truncheons ever-ready to swing into action at the first sign of trouble.

"This way," said my warder curtly.

I followed him through the crush of people at the tables, until we came to a table where a boy was sitting. It was Ketch from the workhouse.

"You've got ten minutes," said the warder. "Keep your hands on the table where we can see them at all times."

Then the warder moved away.

I was aware that every warder was watching everyone and everything. Even the slightest attempt by one woman to reach out and touch the hand of the man opposite was swiftly stopped by a shout of "No touching!"

I sat down opposite Ketch.

"What's up?" I asked.

Ketch looked around furtively, then leaned forward and whispered: "I got a message for you."

I waited.

Ketch looked around again, and then looked at me and said: "A certain gentlemen says if you mention his name it'll be the worse for you. And he knows people in here." His

74

voice dropped even lower and I had to strain to make out the words as he whispered: "Officers who owe him. He says, keep your mouth shut and he'll see what he can do. But say his name, and you're dead for sure."

With that Ketch got up. Immediately a warder arrived by our table.

"Finished?" he demanded.

"Yes, sir," nodded Ketch.

"Prisoner to be returned to cell!" called the warder.

The warder who'd brought me to the visiting room made his way to the table.

"Right, you," he snapped. "Come on."

I stood up and followed him back through the bustle of the visiting room to the heavy wooden door. The warder on duty unlocked it, and we walked through, back into the stone-floored corridor.

The door shut behind us and was locked, and then I walked back beside the warder to my cell. So that had been my visitor. A warning from Hutch, Griffin and Drutt. Keep quiet or you'll be killed by the warders inside the prison. Hutch seemed to have a lot of people in his pay. I looked at the warder walking beside me and wondered if he might be one of the officers Ketch had spoken about?

We arrived back at my cell where the turnkey unlocked the door and I walked in. The metal door clanged shut behind me.

I walked over to the bunk with the thin mattress and sat down on it, and wept; tears pouring out of me.

I was going to die. I was so young, and none of this was my fault, and I was going to die.

Chapter fifteen

The next day I was allowed out into the exercise yard with the other prisoners for half an hour. After the gloom and loneliness of the cell, it was nice to see daylight again, and people other than warders and turnkeys.

I'd been told by the warders that I was only allowed in a certain part of the yard, and that was where I had to stay while I was out exercising. Our half of the yard was called the Commons area, and was for poor prisoners.

The other half of the yard was called the State area, and that was where prisoners walked who had money. These richer prisoners also had better cells and got better food than the poor prisoners, but they had to pay for it. There were a lot more prisoners in my part of the yard, the Commons area, but I didn't mind that. The more there were, the more I could hide myself in the crowd away from the watching eyes of the warders for a few precious minutes.

It was strange being in that yard and looking at the different prisoners. In our part of the yard, the Commons, there were all sorts: men, women and children, and the one thing they all had in common was they looked ragged and poor. Most of them had battered-looking faces, even the women.

In the other part of the yard, the State, the prisoners were mostly men and they strolled about or stood and chatted as if they were free men, just out for a casual walk. There wasn't the same look of misery about them as there was with the prisoners on the Commons area. I wondered what those rich people had done to find themselves in Newgate? I bet none of them were in for being burglars.

I was going to hang. Either that, or Hutch would have me killed. Either way I was going to die, as long as I stayed here in Newgate.

As I stood there I looked at the high wall surrounding the yard, and suddenly a wild idea came to me. I'd got into this terrible situation because Griffin had seen me climbing the wall at the workhouse to try and get away. Maybe I could get out of it the same way, by climbing a wall. This wall.

I studied it. It was about 50 feet high – much higher than the wall around the workhouse yard. It was made of granite: lumps of rough stone, rather than bricks. That meant there ought to be more handholds and places where I could put my feet.

One big problem was the metal spikes just below the top of the wall. They were on a long iron bar that ran right along the whole length of the wall, and continued on round the other walls. I'd seen those sort of spiked bars in other places. They were made so that the spikes were in a wheel, pointing in different directions. If anyone touched them the wheel spun so there were always spikes sticking out. You couldn't get a proper grip on them or use them as a foothold. And the sharp points of the spikes were almost touching the wall, so you couldn't squeeze between the spikes and the wall to get round them.

And I guessed that there also were sharp bits of glass stuck into the cement at the very top of the wall.

I carried on walking around the yard, trying to look as if I was just there for the exercise. All the time I was scanning the walls, looking for the best way up. Although the bits of granite stuck out, I could see that in places there were stretches where it was very smooth. Granite is a smooth stone, not like brick. If you get a big stretch of granite it's impossible to get a grip on it, there's nowhere to dig your fingers in; the stone is just too hard and slippery.

Then I saw a place where I might be able to do it. It was at a corner of the yard where two of the walls joined. About 30 feet from the ground above the corner there was what looked like part of a water cistern jutting out. It didn't jut out much, but if I could get to that I might be able to use it to clamber up to the bar with the iron spikes.

Getting over the spikes would be hard. But not as hard as dying.

The next question was: where did I go after I'd got to the top of the wall? For one thing, I didn't know what was on the other side of that section of wall. If it just dropped straight down to the street, there'd be warders and police waiting for me there.

I looked around the yard some more. The top of that wall continued round to another section of wall. My hope was that there'd be buildings nearby. If I could get to them, to the roofs of those buildings, I might be able to get away.

It was a chance, but one thing was sure: if I stayed in Newgate I'd die. I'd either be hanged as a burglar, or if I saved my neck by giving the police Hutch's name, I'd be killed by his people.

As I was standing in the yard, thinking about this, there was the sound of a whistle, and everyone stood still.

"Exercise over!" shouted a warder. "Back to your cells!"

Time was up. It was now or never.

There was a second whistle, and everyone began to trudge slowly towards the doors that led back into the cells. I headed the other way, towards the corner where the two walls joined, and where the cistern was. I was lucky. The warders were concentrating on the prisoners heading towards the doors and didn't spot me at first. I reached the corner and looked up, spotting the handholds, and then began to climb.

"Oi! That boy!"

There was a shout from one of the warders, and then the sound of a whistle blowing. First it was blown twice to make everyone stop, and then it blew three times to raise the alarm. The realization that the warders were running towards where I was spurred me on and I climbed higher, pressing myself into the corner, scrabbling up the granite as fast as I could, doing my best to keep calm and not panic. If I panicked I might lose my footing and fall, and it would be all over for me.

Below me there were more whistles and more shouts from warders, but now the sound in their voices was more urgent as I got nearer the cistern. Then suddenly I heard a shout of, "Go on, boy! Climb!" and someone gave a cheer. And then someone else joined in the cheer, and someone else called, "Go! Go!" and more voices joined in shouting and urging me on. At that, more whistles were blown, but the shouting and jeering just got louder. Then there was the sound of scuffles and yells of pain, and I could tell that the warders had begun attacking the prisoners with their truncheons. Then the shouting and yelling got louder, and this time the voices were a mixture: men, women and children.

I took the chance to look down. The exercise yard had turned into a riot, with warders trying to get the prisoners back to their cells, and the prisoners refusing to go. Fights were breaking out. More whistles were blown, and more warders poured into the yard.

This was good news for me because the more warders and officers there were trying to stop the riot in the yard, the fewer there would be available to get outside the walls of the prison to catch me as I came down outside.

I looked up and continued my climb, heading for the cistern. Higher and higher I went, gripping onto the tops of the pieces of granite with my fingertips, and pressing the toes of my boots into the cracks in the wall. My fingers were aching from the strain of holding on, and my ankles and calves were crying out with pain from the effort of keeping footholds, but I daren't let go or relax my hold. If I did I'd fall to the ground, which was now about 25 feet below, and I'd be killed for certain. The cistern was about five feet above me now. I pushed and pulled my way up the wall, and at last managed to get a hold on the top of the cistern and haul myself up.

I rested my bottom on the top of the cistern, and for a moment I was able to let my fingers and legs recover. But I knew I didn't have long. I wondered if even now the warders or police might be fetching ladders to try to follow me up the wall.

The bar with the metal spikes on was about another ten feet above me, and the top of the wall another ten feet higher than that.

Below me in the prison yard the shouts and yells and fighting continued.

I stood up carefully on the top of the cistern, my hands

pressing against the wall to keep my balance. Then I began to climb again. Up, up, up I went, the same as before: fingertips clinging on to the jutting-out stones; toes finding nooks and cracks in the wall.

Finally I was at the iron bar. I reached up and touched one of the metal spikes, and felt it spin loose on its axle. As it spun, the sharp point of the spike slashed through the skin on my hand, making it bleed. There was no other way. I had to get over these spikes. I'd just have to try and close off my mind against any pain.

I managed to find handholds on the bar between the revolving spikes, and I hauled myself up, pushing with my feet against the wall. All the way up, the spikes tore at my clothes and chest. They were only surface scratches, but they hurt as if salt had been rubbed into them, and blood was speckling my shirt. I daren't stop now. Death awaited me if I stopped. I gritted my teeth against the pain and pushed upwards. I felt one of the revolving spikes tear into my thigh, deeper than the other cuts. The pain made me feel sick and I had to bite my lip to stop myself crying out.

I climbed onto the top of the bar, and again managed to get footholds between the spikes. It was lucky I was small. An adult wouldn't have been able to get their feet onto the bar in this way.

Once again I balanced myself against the wall, only now my hands left bloodstains where they touched the wall.

I resumed my climb. The top of the wall was just a few feet above me now. Painfully, my hands and legs in agony both from the terrible strain I was putting on my muscles and from the cuts in my hands, chest and thighs, I inched my way up the wall. Six feet to go. Five. Four. Three. Two. Nearly there. One foot to go. I reached up, and my fingers found the top of the wall. I felt sharp pain, and realized that there was broken glass stuck into the cement at the top of the wall, as I'd guessed. Despite the glass, I dragged myself up, onto the top of the wall.

The wall was about eighteen inches wide. I sat on top of it, trying to ignore the pain from the broken glass.

Inside the prison, the riot was being brought under control. There were fewer prisoners now; most had been taken back to their cells. I looked down the other side of the wall, at the outside. As I had feared, warders and police constables were already there in the street, looking up at me.

"Stay there, boy!" one called up to me. "We've sent for a long ladder! Give yourself up!"

I looked along the wall. It ran for about 50 yards, and then turned at a right angle and continued for another 50 yards, before turning again at another right angle and heading back towards the prison buildings. Directly below me was an open street, which was now filling up with police and warders, while more police battled to hold back the crowds who'd come to watch the excitement.

I looked towards the prison buildings, and saw that near their roofs were other roofs. The roofs of buildings that were outside the prison. If I could reach one of them, I could get away!

I stood up, and for the first time I felt a sudden gust of wind tug at me and nearly knock me off the top of the wall and back down into the prison yard. I sat down again and held on to the top of the wall. This was going to be dangerous. If I stood up and walked, then the wind might blow me off the wall. But if I crawled along the wall I would tear my hands and knees to ribbons on the shards of broken glass. I was already bleeding from the cuts I'd got so far.

I needed to get to those distant roofs as quickly as I could, before the long ladders arrived.

I took a decision. My boots would protect my feet against the glass. I'd walk along the narrow top of the wall and hope that I could hold my balance against any more strong gusts of wind.

I set off, going as fast as I could, my arms held out on either side to help me keep my balance. I couldn't go too fast because the top of the wall was uneven. With the cement and the glass underfoot, it would be very easy to trip and fall.

I was aware of more shouting below, and realized the police were following me in the street below. A couple of times I stumbled and nearly fell, but I stopped and got my balance back, took a deep breath to calm myself, and then continued walking.

I reached the junction in the wall. The next section also backed on to a street. By now the noise from the streets below was incredible: a babble of yells and shouts. The news of what I was doing had obviously spread around this area of London, and now the police had the problem of trying to keep the crowds at bay.

I made it to the next corner. The top of the next stretch of wall led straight to the roof of the prison building. Again, it was about eighteen inches wide and 50 yards long. I set off once more, trying to keep my balance on the uneven cement and the bits of sharp glass sticking up. A gust of wind hit me again, and I wobbled and nearly fell, but I managed to regain my balance. I was nearly there. Twenty yards to go. Ten.

Then, to my horror, I saw a skylight in the roof of the prison building begin to lift. They were coming after me that way! They had managed to get a ladder up to the skylight! At any moment warders would be out on the roof!

I tried to run, but it was too dangerous. All I could do was go a bit faster. I had to reach the roof before the warders came out. What I was going to do when I got there, I didn't know. But I just knew I had to get there. Once I was there, I might stand a chance of getting away.

The edge of the skylight was lifting slowly upwards, and

then it fell back down. I guessed that skylight hadn't been opened in years and the joint was rusty. I knew that one hard push and it would fly open. But it had given me a few seconds of valuable time.

As I saw the skylight window move up again, I made a last rush and almost fell off the wall onto the slates of the roof.

Panting, I lay there, holding on to the slates and looking around. The prison building was separated from the next building by an alleyway. The gap between the two roofs was about nine feet. I had no chance of taking a run at the gap because of the slope of the roof I was on. The roof opposite also sloped, down towards the alley. Even if I made the jump and got to the other roof, there was a chance I would slide off and fall down into the alley, about 50 feet below.

There was a sudden crashing noise behind me, and I turned and saw that the window of the skylight had now been forced open. A prison warder was clambering out through the opening on to the roof, and I knew he wouldn't be alone.

I looked across to the roof on the other side of the alley. A distance of nine feet from a standing start on slippery sloping tiles. And I was worn out and aching and in pain, with the weight of my boots dragging me down.

"Stop there, boy!" shouted a voice.

I turned. There were two warders out on the roof now, with the head of a third already poking out through the skylight window.

To jump? Or stay, and be taken prisoner again, and be sure to hang?

I gritted my teeth, took a deep breath, and jumped.

Chapter sixteen

For what felt like ages I seemed to hang in empty air, and then I crashed into the tiles of the roof opposite. I hit them with such force that I began to slide downwards and felt myself fall off the edge of the roof. Just in time I managed to grab hold of the guttering. Straining with all my strength, I pulled myself up until I could swing a foot up into the iron gutter. Using that as a foothold, I was able to struggle up and get back onto the roof.

The warders were clinging to the chimney of the prison building and didn't look like they were about to follow me and jump across the gap. One of them shouted angrily: "You won't get away!"

Then two of them disappeared back down through the skylight, leaving one to watch what I did and where I went.

I knew I didn't have long. The police would be rushing into all the buildings this side of the alleyway, searching them, trying to cut off my escape. I had to get as far away as possible from the building I was on, and fast.

Luckily the skills I'd built up as a burglar, scrambling and clambering over roofs, helped me. I moved as quickly as I could, sometimes slipping and sliding on the roof slates. All the time my body was crying out with the pain from the bleeding cuts in my hands and my aching muscles.

I had to get off the roofs. As long as I stayed here the police could see me. I had to get inside somewhere.

Then I saw an open skylight. I didn't know where it led to, I just knew it was a way off the roof. I hurried over to it and looked in. There was no one in sight inside. The smell of washing soda and wet clothes told me this was some kind of laundry. If I could get down and through it and out to the street without anyone seeing me, I'd be able to get away to safety.

I balanced myself on the edge of the skylight, just as I'd done when I was burgling houses, then I swung myself down and let myself drop. My whole body ached with pain as I hit the floor.

I got up and headed for the stairs. I made it down the first flight of stairs without anyone seeing me. I heard voices from behind the closed doors of different rooms off the stairs and landings. So long as they stayed closed, I would be all right.

Down I went, one flight of stairs after another. I knew I was nearly at the ground floor. Just a few more paces and I'd be safe.

Suddenly a door near me opened and a young girl, carrying a load of washing all neatly ironed, stepped out in front of me. She saw me and let out a scream and dropped all her ironing.

"Please!" I began to beg, urging her to keep quiet, but it was too late. Doors around me opened and women hurried out, eyes expectant, wondering what had made the girl scream. One woman took a look at me and her mouth dropped open.

"My Lord!" she breathed. "Look at him! He's been murdered!"

Then I realized how I must have looked to the girl and the woman, with blood staining the front of my shirt, and blood and dirt elsewhere on me. I looked like I'd been the victim of a serious attack.

"No…" I began again.

"Call the police!" said one woman.

Again I pleaded "No!" but in a much desperate tone this time.

There were about seven women now gathered around me, all looking at me, astonished. Then one of them said: "It must be him who's escaped from Newgate! They were talking about it in the street! He climbed the wall and jumped off the roof!"

Even as she said it, I heard a banging at the front door and a voice calling out: "Police! Open up!"

My heart sank. To have got this far, and be caught after all the pain and danger I'd gone through.

One of the woman stepped towards the front door, but then another woman hissed out urgently: "No, Sadie! Wait!" As Sadie and the other women looked at her, she said:

"You and Queenie take him downstairs to the washing room and stick him in a laundry sack. Then stick a load of other dirty laundry sacks on top of him. And be quick!"

"Right, Vi," nodded Sadie.

The banging at the front door sounded again, louder, and the voice was more insistent: "Open this door at once! Police! Official business!"

"All right, we're coming!" called Vi. "Keep your shirt on!"

I had a glimpse of Vi heading towards the door, then Sadie and the girl, Queenie, hustled me down the stone steps to the washing room.

The washing room was a large stone room in the basement with loads of big sinks along one wall, and a large copper tank built over a grate, in which a fire was burning. The place smelt of steam and wet clothing. Sacks of dirty washing were stacked up along one of the walls. Sadie picked up one of the big sacks and emptied the dirty washing out onto the floor, then handed it to me.

"Go to that corner and get inside this. Quick!"

I pulled the sack over my head and then lay down in the corner. I had barely got myself on the floor when I felt other sacks being dumped on top of me. Sadie and Queenie were piling sacks onto me as fast as they could. I hoped they wouldn't put too many on me. It would be awful if I had managed to escape this far, and then suffocated to death under the weight of all this dirty washing.

The dumping of bags on me stopped, and I could make out the sound of boots coming down the stone steps, and Vi saying, "I don't care who you're looking for, you'd better not make a mess of our laundry. There's a lot of washing here belongs to important people."

Then a male voice said: "We're only doing our duty. This boy is dangerous."

"Is he a murderer?" asked Sadie in an awed voice, and I hoped she wouldn't do or say anything that might arouse the police's suspicions.

"He may be," said the police officer.

"What do you mean, he *may* be?" demanded Vi. And there was no mistaking the annoyance in her voice. "Don't you know?"

"We're not sure," said the policeman. "All we know is he's an escaped prisoner, so that makes him dangerous. That's why we've got orders to search every building." Then he asked: "What's in those sacks?"

I felt a cold chill go through me. He was obviously pointing at the pile of sacks of laundry where I was hiding.

"Dirty laundry," said Vi. "Take a look, if you want." My heart sank further as she said this. Then she gave a chuckle. "If you don't mind a bit of disease."

"What do you mean?" asked the policeman, and there was a note of unease in his voice.

"Those sacks are from the hospital," said Vi. "Bed sheets

93

and the like. They've had a bit of an epidemic." She sighed. "Cholera is terrible."

"Cholera?!" The constable was shocked. "You mean they've sent you sheets contaminated with cholera?!"

"Well, they *say* they're not," said Vi. "But then, they would, wouldn't they. I mean, I know they're supposed to burn them, but sheets cost money, and no one's got money to waste these days. Anyway, feel free to open 'em up and dig your hands in."

"No, that's all right," said the policeman. "If you say he never came down here, that's good enough for me."

There was the sound of another pair of heavy boots coming down the steps, then a new voice said: "No sign of him anywhere upstairs, Sarge."

"All right," said the police officer. "Move on to the next building."

Then there was the sound of the heavy boots going back up the stone steps.

I stayed where I was inside the sack, keeping still in case he changed his mind and came back. But he must have really gone, because I felt the other sacks being lifted off me. I pulled the sack off and looked at Vi, Sadie, Queenie, and the other women who had now all gathered in the washing room and were looking at me.

"Thank you," I said. "I'm not a murderer. Honest."

"I know," said Vi. "I can tell."

"The reason I was in Newgate—" I began.

Vi stopped me.

"Tell us later," she said. "Right now we'd clean up those cuts of yours before they turn septic. And then we can work out what we're going to do with you."

Chapter seventeen

I could tell by the expressions on some of their faces that a few of the washerwomen were suspicious of me, but it was also obvious that Vi was in charge, and what she said went. They took my blood-stained and torn clothes, and then let me wash myself in the hot water from the copper. Then another of the women, Daisy, brought out some paste which she painted on my cuts.

"This'll help 'em heal and stop 'em going septic," she told me. "It's an old herbal remedy my Gran passed on to me." Then she bandaged my hands.

Vi produced a new set of clothes for me: shirt, trousers and a jacket. They were old and worn, but clean and my size.

"Leftovers," she said. "They'll do you for the moment."

Meanwhile, Sadie had been out and bought a bowl of hot pease pudding, and she gave it to me. It was the first proper food I'd had for ages and I was so hungry I spooned it down, ignoring the pain from the cuts on my hands. In fact, they were beginning to feel better already. I wondered if it was Daisy's Gran's herbal paste, or just getting hot food inside me.

After I'd eaten and was washed and dressed, Vi sat me

down on a chair in the washing room and the other women gathered round to look at me. With what had happened today, I was a real curiosity.

"Is it true you climbed the wall to get out?" asked Vi.

I nodded.

"That's how I got the cuts," I explained. "From the spikes and the glass on the top of the wall."

"What were you in for?" asked Queenie, and her eyes were big in amazement as she looked at me.

"Now that's not a very polite question to ask, Queenie," Vi reprimanded her.

"No, that's all right," I said. "You helped me. You deserve to know. The police caught me for burglary. But I didn't want to do it. I was forced by this man. I used to be a chimney boy, which is why he forced me to be a burglar. But I never wanted to do it. And I never hurt anyone. And he said he'd kill me if I told anyone about him. I had to get out of prison or they'd hang me."

Vi looked at me and frowned.

"They don't hang you for burgling," she said.

"They used to," pointed out one of the other women. "My neighbour's father-in-law got hanged for it."

"Yeah, but they stopped that years ago. Now you just get hard labour."

I stared at the women, stunned.

"But … they told me I'd get hanged."

"Who did?" asked Vi.

"Everyone," I said. "Even the detective who arrested me."

Vi shook her head.

"He was just frightening you," she told me. "Trying to scare you into giving them the name of the bloke you worked for. Anyway, you can't stay here."

"He can't stay in this area, either," added Sadie. "The police will be poking around asking questions all over, looking for him. Someone's bound to spot him."

"The longer he's here the more dangerous it'll be for him," said Daisy.

"And for us," put in another woman. "We'll all go to Newgate for harbouring an escaped convict."

At these words a silence fell over everyone. Even Vi looked worried at the thought. Then she nodded, as if she'd come to a decision.

"You're right, Molly," she said. "He's got to get away from here right now. Get away from the whole area."

"But the police are watching for him!" protested Queenie. "The streets are packed with coppers, all looking for him!"

"I bet they've put a cordon round the whole place," said Daisy.

"And if they catch him trying to get away, they're going to work out where he got those clothes," said Molly. "And we'll all be in big trouble."

Once more, Vi nodded thoughtfully.

"In that case, it's best if you don't know what I'm going to do with him," she told them. "So, all of you get on with your work. I shall be going out for a bit when I've finished down here."

Queenie looked puzzled.

"But what *are* you going to do with him?" she asked.

"Like Vi said, better none of us knows," Sadie told her. "Come on, girls. Back to work!"

Vi waited until the other women had gone upstairs. Queenie tried to stay behind in the washing room by saying she had sacks to empty, but Vi sent her upstairs very firmly with the others. Then she turned to me.

"Right," she said. "You can't stay anywhere in this area. Your best bet is to get to the East End, over Whitechapel way. It's far enough away from here and very crowded. All sorts of people live there. The police do their best not to walk around the East End if they can help it, even in pairs. You'll be safer there than here, providing you keep your head down."

"But how am I going to get to the East End?" I asked. "Like everyone said, the police will be out in force looking for me. Every street will be filled with police."

Vi gave a funny smile.

"The police are looking for a beggar boy with bloodstained clothes. They won't be looking for a girl out with her mum."

I gaped at her.

"A girl?"

Vi nodded.

"We'll put a long dress on over your own clothes. A big bonnet will hide your hair and your face. Once we get to the East End I'll take the dress and bonnet back off you, and then you're on your own."

I shook my head defiantly.

"I'm not dressing up as a girl!" I said firmly.

Vi shrugged.

"Please yourself," she said. I stood there, looking at her, my mind in a whirl. Then I gave a sigh and a shrug.

"All right," I said.

Chapter eighteen

We walked along Newgate Street into Cheapside, then along Poultry and Cornhill, heading east towards Whitechapel. All the time I kept my head down so the bonnet hid my face, because there was no way I was going to pass as a girl.

When we first left the laundry, my heart was thumping and I could barely breathe for fear we were going to be caught. Police were everywhere, like a swarm of bees. They were stopping all the boys in the streets around Newgate and getting them to hold out their hands so they could see if any of them had cuts on them. Luckily for me, Vi had made sure I put on a pair of gloves to cover my bandages.

Vi insisted we kept moving fast.

"Look like we're on our way somewhere," she instructed me. "That way they're less likely to stop us and ask if we've seen anything. No one likes to get a mouthful from a woman who's in a hurry and is being stopped to be asked stupid questions."

We kept up a fast pace: Vi striding along, carrying an empty bag, and me hurrying along beside her. On the few occasions when I thought a policeman looked in our direction and might be about to stop us and ask us anything, Vi turned and snapped angrily at me: "For heaven's sake, girl, stop dawdling! We've got to get home before your Dad gets back!"

The angry tone of her voice, and the fact that we were mother and daughter, made them decide to let us pass.

Vi had told me to keep my mouth shut as we walked, and I did. I finally felt able to say something as we neared Whitechapel. By this time we had passed through the areas where the police were out in force, and for the last fifteen minutes we hadn't even seen a policeman. As Vi had said, the police weren't keen on walking around in a tough area like Whitechapel.

"Why are you helping me?" I asked. It had puzzled me from the moment they hid me in the sack among the dirty laundry.

"Why shouldn't we?" said Vi, and she kept walking.

"Yes, but you put yourself at risk," I pointed out. "You could have gone to jail if we'd been caught."

Vi didn't reply at once, just kept on walking, keeping up the same fast pace she'd set when we first left the laundry. Finally she said: "I had a son once. He'd be about your age. Maybe a bit older."

"What happened to him?" I asked, curious.

She shook her head.

"None of your business," she said.

She stopped.

"Right. Here we are. Whitechapel. You're on your own

102

from here." She gestured towards an alley, and handed me the bag she was carrying. "Nip in there and take off the dress and bonnet. Put 'em in the bag."

I did as she said. When I returned and gave her the bag, she held out a paper parcel to me.

"Here," she said. "There's a pie and a bit of cheese in there. That'll keep you going for a bit."

"Thanks," I said.

I looked around me.

"I've never been to this part of London before," I said.

"It's rough," she said. "Keep your head down and the police shouldn't bother you." She looked up at the roofs of the buildings. "I hear there's lots of runaway kids who live on the roofs because the chimneys keep 'em warm. Find a gang of 'em. That's my advice. There's safety in numbers."

"Thanks," I said.

Suddenly I felt choked up. In all my life Vi was the first person who'd been really nice to me. She'd put herself at serious risk for me. And now she was going and I'd never see her again.

"Here, don't start crying," said Vi. "You'll be all right, providing you're careful."

I felt ashamed of myself for letting her see that I was almost crying. I bit my lip to stop the tears from rolling out.

"It's not that," I said. "You're the first person I've ever met who's been good to me in any way."

"Then pass it on," said Vi. "Help someone else."

She went to go, and then she stopped and looked at me.

"His name's Norman," she said. And now I saw there were tears in her eyes. "Norman Adams. He'd be 11. If you see him, tell him where I am."

Then she turned away again and hurried off, her head down. I watched her go, watched her disappear among the crowds of people. And then I turned and walked into Whitechapel.

Chapter nineteen

Even though Whitechapel is part of London, it was like another country. Or, lots of countries. There were people of all different colours talking all sorts of languages, and dressed in so many different kinds of costumes. Chinese with their hair tied in pigtails, Jews with their hair curled in long ribbons sticking out from under big-brimmed hats. People with black skins, with brown skins. And all manner of accents. Some I recognized as Irish because Camden Town, where I came from, was full of Irish people. But some of the accents were puzzling and I couldn't work out what people were saying. I suppose it was because we weren't far from the docks, and most people who'd come here from other countries had decided to stay near where they'd arrived.

The streets of Whitechapel were different, too. Muddier. Most of the roads around where I came from were cobbled. A lot of the streets here were just earth, churned up by horses, carts and people. And they seemed narrower, too, with some of the roofs of the buildings on opposite sides of the streets and alleys almost touching.

By now it was getting late. Darkness would be falling soon.

I needed to find somewhere to sleep where I'd be safe. Vi had talked about gangs of runaway children living on the roofs. I guessed that she meant the flat roofs of factories, rather than houses where people lived. Factory roofs would also be safer because there'd be no one in the building at night to kick the kids off.

Most of the children wouldn't be climbers like me, so there must be ladders or staircases that went up to some of the roofs. The question was, where would I find them? This area was strange to me. With the narrow alleys going in all directions it was like a maze. I could walk around it for hours and not find what I was looking for.

I stopped a man in the street, and took a chance he understood and spoke English.

"Sorry, sir," I said. "I'm looking for factory work. Can you tell me where the factories are?"

The man looked down at me and laughed.

"Looking for work?" he chuckled. "That's a good one! Looking for a place to hide, more than likely."

"No!" I protested.

The man shook his head.

"Don't worry. It's none of my business. But if you're looking for a factory, they're all up there," and he pointed towards a narrow lane. "Match factory, boot-blacking factory. Clothes. Leather. You name it, that's where you'll find them."

"Thank you, sir," I said.

He laughed again. "You'll soon recognize 'em because of all the kids living on the roofs."

With that he walked off, still chuckling to himself.

I walked into the alley he had pointed at. I was puzzled. If everyone knew there were loads of runaway children living on the roofs of the factories, why wasn't anyone doing anything about it? Why didn't the factory owners get rid of them? Why weren't they rounded up and put into workhouses?

I followed the alleyway, and then it opened up into a wider street. Here there weren't so many crowds. It was getting dark. I supposed most of the people who worked at the factories had gone home.

I saw small shapes moving in the shadows of the street, and the alleys and lanes that went off it. Children. But how did they get up to the roofs?

Then I saw two small children hurry out of one alleyway and disappear round the back of one of the large factory buildings. I hurried after them, doing my best not to let them know I was following them.

I reached the corner of the building and peered round. The two children, a boy and a girl, had stopped by a metal staircase that went up and up to the roof of the building.

I let the two children go up, and waited until they had vanished from sight at the top before I followed them. I didn't want the sound of my boots on the metal stairs to alarm them.

I wondered who they were, and I wondered how many of them there were. Were they all just children, or were there adults with them? It suddenly struck me that maybe this gang of children on this particular roof might be part of a criminal gang, with a vicious hard criminal with them. Someone like Hutch. In which case, I'd be going into danger.

This thought made me stop, and for a moment I thought about turning round and going back down the stairs. But if I did that, where would I go? Another roof? And maybe walk into another dangerous situation? I was already in a dangerous situation. I was an escaped convict. As Vi had said, I needed to find safety, and that meant finding a gang of kids. I would just have to take my chance.

I kept on going, up the metal fire escape, until I came to the roof. I peered over the top of the edge of the roof. There was no one in sight, but I could hear voices coming from behind the stack of chimneys.

I climbed onto the roof and tiptoed towards the sound of voices, doing my best to keep in the shadows thrown by the tall chimney stacks so I wouldn't be seen.

I reached the chimneys and pressed myself into the brickwork, straining to hear what was being said and who was there.

Suddenly I felt myself gripped from behind by powerful arms and a boy's voice snapped out: "Kill him! Chuck him off the roof!"

Chapter twenty

"No!" shouted a girl's voice. "Bring him out here!"

I managed to turn my head a bit, and saw that the person holding me was a big boy of about fourteen. He was tall and very tough looking, with enormous hands. Standing next to him was a much smaller, rat-faced boy who was glaring at me with venom in his eyes. I guessed it had been he who'd told the big boy to throw me off the roof.

A short thin girl was standing looking at me.

"Come on," she said impatiently. "Bring him out where we can all see him!"

The smaller boy spat in annoyance, but moved aside. The bigger boy ushered me past the chimneys, but still kept a firm grip on one of my arms, his powerful fingers digging painfully into the muscle just below my shoulder.

I saw that there were six children gathered on the roof. All of them were looking at me.

"He's a spy!" said the small boy who'd glared at me before.

"No I ain't," I protested.

"Then what were you doing eavesdropping on us like that?" demanded the girl.

"I was looking for a place to sleep. Someone told me the roofs were the best place."

The small boy laughed sarcastically.

"Yeah! The police!" he sneered. "He's a spy!" He reached out and took hold of my jacket. "Just look at this. Clean clothes. What sort of runaway has clean clothes?"

"They were given to me by a laundrywoman," I said.

"Why?" demanded the girl.

I hesitated. If I told them what had happened, they might turn me in. There was bound to be a reward out for me. But if I didn't, they'd think I was a spy. I decided to tell them half the story.

"I ran away," I said. "I had an accident. My clothes were all messy and torn. Some women in a laundry took me in, but they couldn't keep me because of the people who were looking for me. So they gave me these clothes."

"Who was looking for you?" demanded the small, rat-faced boy.

"You don't half ask a lot of questions, Jim!" said the girl.

"You got to know who you're dealing with, Amy," insisted Jim, still regarding me suspiciously.

The girl, Amy, looked at my bandaged hands.

"What did you do to your hands?" she asked.

"I cut them," I answered.

"How?"

"Climbing a wall."

"Oh yeah!" sneered Jim. "I bet that's another trick so we can't see he's got soft hands." To the big boy who was still holding me, he said: "Joe, hold him tight while I take off one of these bandages."

"That's not right!" protested the smaller girl. "You might hurt him!"

"Hurt him, Vicky?" mocked Jim. "He's pretending! Trust me!"

While Joe held my arm, I let Jim tear off the bandage from one of my hands. He was rough doing it, as if he was enjoying it and looking forward to exposing me as a fraud. The pain made me want to cry out, but I was determined not to give him that pleasure. As the last of the bandage came off and exposed my hand, torn and slashed with cuts from the glass and the iron spikes, the expression on his face changed dramatically.

"God's truth!" he exclaimed.

At the shock in his voice, the other kids gathered round to look.

Amy looked at my hand, and then at me.

"That must hurt a lot," she said.

"It does," I said.

"Why didn't you cry out when Jim was tearing the bandage off?" she demanded. "He must have hurt you."

"He did," I said. "But I've had worse."

Amy turned her attention to the big boy who was still holding me.

"Let him go, Joe," she said.

Immediately, Joe let go of my arm, and I felt a sense of relief.

The small girl who'd spoken before pointed to my other hand.

"Is that one as bad?" she asked.

I nodded.

"A bit worse," I answered. I turned to Jim. "If you'd treated the other hand the same way, I might have cried out then."

"It wasn't my fault!" protested Jim. "You looked like a spy!"

"OK," nodded Amy. "You can join us. What's your name?"

"Will."

"Right, Will. I'm Amy. And I'm in charge. What I say goes. Right?"

I was slightly taken aback at this. Amy was smaller and thinner than Joe, and looked a lot less dangerous than Jim. But they obviously accepted her as the leader of their gang.

I nodded. "Right," I said.

"I'll introduce you to the rest. Jim and Joe you've already met."

Jim looked uncomfortable.

"Yeah," he said. "I'm sorry I got you wrong. OK?"

"OK," I said.

I looked at the huge figure of Joe. Big and muscular,

but there was something in his face that showed he had trouble thinking. He didn't so much looked puzzled as … well, blank.

Amy was introducing the others. She pointed to the small girl who'd protested about Jim hurting me. "That's Vicky." She pointed at a boy who looked about six years old: "That's Paul. Next to him is Mick." A boy who looked a bit older, maybe seven, waved and smiled shyly at me.

"And that's Emma over there." The last was a girl I hadn't spotted before. She was lying on a piece of cloth near the chimney. She had a scarf wrapped round the bottom part of her face which was tied at the back. Emma raised a hand to me in greeting.

"Emma don't speak," said Amy. "Right. That's us. Have you eaten?"

I produced the paper bag Vi had given me.

"I've got a pie and a piece of cheese," I said.

Amy held out her hand.

"Hand it over," she said.

I put my hand protectively over my pocket where the bag was.

"It's mine," I protested.

"Not if you're going to be part of us," said Amy. "We share and share alike. Food. Money. It all goes into the pot and we share it out equal. That's our rule."

I looked around at the others. I felt really disappointed.

I'd been looking forward to sinking my teeth into that pie and piece of cheese.

"It's up to you," shrugged Amy. "If you don't like it, you can go."

I thought of life out on the streets of Whitechapel. Of trying to find another place to stay tonight, where I'd be safe. I sighed. All right, they could share my food tonight. I could always leave them tomorrow and find somewhere else.

I pulled the paper bag from my pocket and handed it to Amy.

"Here," I said.

"Good," smiled Amy. Turning to the others, she said, "Right. Let's eat!"

Chapter twenty-one

I was surprised by how much food the other kids produced from their pockets and bags. Vicky had two large, fat cooked sausages. Mick had some broken biscuits and two apples. Paul had a pie. Jim produced a loaf of bread and a bigger piece of cheese than mine. When he saw I noticed that big Joe didn't produce anything, he added for my benefit: "These are from both me and Joe."

I noticed that Emma, the girl with the scarf wrapped round her face, didn't produce any food either, but no one said anything about it.

Amy pulled four slices of cooked ham from her pocket, and the eyes of the kids lit up at the sight of this.

Amy took a knife and cut every piece of food into eight pieces, some a little bigger than the others, but she did the dividing very carefully.

I realized that by adding my pie and piece of cheese into the pot, I'd come out of it with a much better meal. Half a slice of ham, two pieces of pie, two pieces of cheese, a quarter of an apple, a piece of sausage, and some biscuits.

As I tucked in, Jim came and sat down beside me, bringing his food with him.

"I'm sorry about earlier," he said awkwardly. "But we heard that the factory owner wants to get rid of us kids from his roof, and he was sending some thugs to throw us off. I thought you were a spy finding out how many of us there were."

"That's all right," I said. "I expect I'd have done the same." I looked across at where Emma was breaking her food into tiny pieces, and pushing them beneath the scarf tied around her lower face.

"What's wrong with her?" I asked. "Why's she got that scarf tied round her face?"

"Em?" Jim gave an unhappy sigh. "She's got phossy jaw."

I looked at him, puzzled.

"What's phossy jaw?"

Jim looked at me, equally puzzled at my ignorance. Then he realized. "Of course, you ain't from round these parts." He cast a look at Emma and gave her a smile, and then lowered his voice as he explained. "It's what girls who work in match factories get, on account of the phosphorus they use in making matches. It gets into the bone and rots it. In Em's case, it's only the skin of her face, and that scarf, that's holding her jaw in place." He lowered his voice even more, and added in a whisper: "Truth is, she's dying. That's why we don't mind that she don't always bring any food to share for us. She brung us enough when she was well. It's our turn to look after her now."

116

I looked around at the others, all tucking in to the handful of food they had each. Joe sat chewing on his piece of sausage and staring at nothing.

"What about Joe?" I asked.

Jim glared at me angrily.

"Don't you start on Joe!" he growled aggressively.

"I wasn't!" I protested. "I just asked…"

"Well don't," said Jim firmly. He took a bite of his piece of apple, and then said quietly: "Joe saved my life. He saved me from drowning when we was younger. I fell through some ice on the river. Joe jumped in after me and got me out. But he … he got trapped under the ice." Jim looked across at Joe and for a moment I could swear I saw tears in his eyes. Jim chewed on his apple a bit more, then added: "Joe swallowed a lot of water before they got him out. He couldn't breathe properly. Something … happened to his brain." Then Jim's eyes hardened fiercely. "But if anyone did anything to Joe, or made fun of him, I'd kill 'em. I swear!"

"I wasn't making fun!" I protested. "I just wanted to know."

"Well, don't," said Jim. "All of us have got our stories from the past which don't need looking into too deeply." He looked deliberately at me. "You as well, I expect, judging by those cuts on your hands."

I nodded.

"Maybe," I agreed.

"And that's the best place to leave them. In the past," said Jim. "What's important is we work together to make sure we stay alive today, for as long as we can."

Chapter twenty-two

The next morning I went out with the other kids to find work. Because Emma was really weak she couldn't go. Amy suggested that Vicky stay on the roof with Emma in case she needed any help.

I wondered what sort of work the kids did out on the streets? I wondered if it was picking oakum, like I'd done in the workhouse. I was worried that they might be caught up in criminal stuff, like pickpocketing or stealing. I had decided that now I'd put the burgling behind me, I wasn't going to do anything criminal ever again.

Luckily, these kids only did work that was legal. Jim and Joe had got a job on a market stall that sold secondhand clothes and things. Joe carried the heavy boxes for the stall owner, and Jim helped the owner sort things depending on their quality: good-quality stuff in one pile, worn-out and broken things in another. It wasn't regular work, only when the stall owner wanted them. But he paid them: mostly in food, but sometimes in actual cash. Jim told me about it as we walked along the street towards the market, along with Joe, Paul and Mick.

"It's clean work at the market," Jim told me. "I used to be a mudlark. That's hard and dirty work."

"What's a mudlark?" I asked.

"It's what it sounds like," said Jim. "You go down to the Thames at low tide and search in the mud for things. All manner of things get washed up, or come out of the sewers. Coins. Bits of jewellery that people drop down a drain; or it falls into the river. That's if you're lucky. Most of the time it's things like lumps of coal, or old bones, or nails. If you get enough you can sell 'em. But it's hard and dirty work. Joe was good at it, though. He could dig deeper in the mud with his big hands than most people. And he never minded getting all covered in mud."

"So why did you stop?" I asked. "Because it was hard and dirty?"

Jim shook his head.

"We kept finding too many dead bodies for my liking. People who'd drowned 'emselves. I was worried we might catch diseases from 'em."

We pushed our way through the crowds, which were getting thicker as we neared the market. "That's where I met Amy," he said. "She was a mudlark, too."

"Where does Amy work now?" I asked.

"She's a crossing sweeper," said Jim. "She's got a patch right on Whitechapel. People give her money for clearing the muck out of the way when they cross the road. She does all right because she does a good job at it. She pays a penny to this woman for using a broom. Amy's saving up to get her own broom, then she'll be able to make even more money. Amy's a hard worker."

"Amy says we mustn't do anything that's against the law," chimed in little Paul. "She says not even for money. She says if we do we'll go to prison and get hanged or transported."

Jim looked at me and winked.

"See what I mean?" he grinned. "Amy makes a wonderful mum for these kids."

"What work do you two do?" I asked Paul and Mick.

"We run errands," said Mick. "The shopkeepers know us and they give us messages to take."

As I listened to them, I felt suddenly useless. Even these little boys of six and seven were bringing money and food in to the gang. What could I do? All I'd ever been was a chimney boy and a burglar. And if Amy felt so strongly about the kids of her gang not being involved in anything criminal, I wasn't going to let them know about the burglary bit.

"What's up?" asked Jim. "You suddenly look miserable."

"I don't know what to work at," I said.

"You can join us," said Jim. "There's always room for another pair of hands at the market, or one of the shops, providing you don't mind getting your hands dirty."

"Whatever it is, I couldn't get any dirtier than I was when I was a chimney boy," I said.

"You were a chimney boy?" Paul asked me excitedly.

"Yes," I said.

"I want to do that!" said Paul.

"Why?" I asked, surprised.

"Because I like hiding in places," said Paul. "And I like climbing things. Watch!"

And he ran to a building nearby and started climbing up the drainpipe; hand over hand, feet pressing against the wall. I shuddered because it reminded me of the climbs I did when I was a burglar.

"Come down from there, Paul!" barked Jim. "Otherwise you'll get us all in trouble."

Paul scrambled back down and we carried on walking.

"You don't want to be a chimney boy, Paul," I said. "It's horrible work. You can't breathe because of the soot. And the bricks inside the chimney tear your skin or burn you. Do something else."

"Well I want to do something with climbing," said Paul. "Maybe I could be a sailor? They climb when they go up the ship's nets to do the sails of the boat. I know because I've seen them."

"Maybe," I said. "But take my advice, Paul, don't be a chimney boy."

For the next week it went on this way: I went off to work at the market with Jim and Joe; Paul and Mick did their job running messages and errands for shopkeepers and stall-holders; and Amy went to her bit of Whitechapel and kept it clean for people crossing the road.

Vicky stayed behind on the roof most of the time now, looking after Em, who was getting so weak she couldn't even sit up. What was worse, she couldn't even eat or drink. Amy tried to make her, but it was no good. It was heart-breaking to see Emma getting worse every day, but there was nothing we could do. We couldn't take her to a doctor because doctors cost money, and a lot more money than the few pennies we were making working. And, as Jim said, no doctor could help her, anyway. The phossy jaw was draining the life out of her, and no amount of money could make her better. All we could do was be there with her so that when she woke up she knew someone was there to hold her hand, or talk to her and let her know she wasn't alone.

On the Monday of my second week with the kids, Emma was worse than usual. She'd started making strange sounds, like she was trying to talk, but she didn't seem to know who was with her.

"I'll stay with her today," Amy told us. "Will, will you do my crossing for me?"

"Of course," I said.

"Take Vicky with you. She knows where my pitch is and

the woman I get the broom from knows Vicky, so she'll let you have it."

And so we went off for the day.

I spent the day sweeping Amy's section of the Whitechapel main road, brushing the horse muck and other dirt out of the path of well-dressed people when they wanted to cross the road, making sure the dirt didn't mess the bottom of the women's long dresses or ruin the gentlemen's trousers. A few of them just pushed past me as they crossed, but most of them gave me a coin. I was earning money honestly.

That evening Vicky and I headed back to the roof. On the way we met up with the others, who were coming from the market. It had been a good day for them. All of them had tales of how they'd been given something by one of the shopkeepers or stall-holders.

"I got a baked potato!" said Paul, holding it up proudly. "It feels really soft inside, so I thought it might be good for Em. She might be able to eat it cos it's soft. It'll be good for her. Soft food."

We got to the top of the fire escape and on to the roof, and I could tell straight away that something was wrong. Amy was kneeling by Em, and Em wasn't moving.

As we arrived, Amy stood up and turned to us.

"Em's dead," said Amy.

Chapter twenty-three

Immediately Vicky and Paul began to cry. Even though I hadn't known Emma long, I felt a lump in my throat. But the main feeling I had in me was anger. Emma shouldn't have died. If she hadn't worked in the match factory she wouldn't have got phossy jaw. If she'd had money and parents, maybe, even after she'd got it, she might have been able to go into a hospital, and maybe they could have found a cure for her. But because she was poor and didn't have anyone to look after her, she died.

Yes, she had Amy and the gang of kids, but all they could do was keep her safe. They couldn't pay for a doctor to look after her, or cure her.

"She worked here," muttered Jim.

"Where?" I asked.

"Here," said Jim, and he tapped the roof with his foot. "At this place. This is the match factory. After Lord Muck kicked her out when she got ill, she came up to the roof because she had nowhere else to go. Her parents were dead, and she didn't have no other family. So we became her family."

"Lord Muck?"

"Lord Martwell," said Jim, and as he said the name he spat a gob of phlegm viciously on the roof. "High and mighty. All he thinks of is making money." He looked across at the body of Emma and his face darkened. "If you ask me, he as good as murdered Em. He shouldn't have let her and the girls work like that, where they got sick. And when they did he should have sent them to a doctor, instead of kicking them out." He scowled, and I could feel his rage as he added vengefully, "I'd like to get my hands on that Lord Martwell! Just ten minutes, that's all I'd need! I'd let him suffer, and then I'd kill him and throw him off this roof!"

"What are we going to do with her?" asked Paul.

He looked lost and helpless, standing there looking at poor dead Emma.

"We can't leave her here," said Amy. She stood there, obviously thinking about it. Finally she said: "We'll carry her downstairs and leave her where someone will find her. They'll have to take her away and bury her. They're not allowed to leave dead people in the street."

"It's rotten!" said Vicky, and she burst into tears. "She ought to have a proper burial!" she sobbed between tears. "With proper words said over her. She won't get into Heaven if she doesn't."

Amy went to Vicky and put her arms around her, cuddling the small sobbing girl to her.

126

"Don't worry, Vicky," she said. "We'll say proper words over her. God will take her into Heaven all right. We'll see to that."

Turning to me, she said, "You and Joe are the biggest and strongest. You two had better carry Emma."

"Where are we going to take her?" I asked. "If anyone sees us dumping her, we'll be in big trouble."

"You just follow me," said Amy. To the others, she said: "If you're frightened to come, you don't have to."

Mick spoke up for the first time.

"I'm not frightened," said Mick. "I want to come."

"Me too," said Paul.

"And m-m-me," nodded Vicky, wiping her eyes, but still crying.

I realized that Jim was no longer with me. He was kneeling down writing something with a bit of chalk on an old piece of cardboard.

"I'm coming as well," he said. "You lot go on. I'll catch you all up. I just gotta do this first."

I walked over to where Emma lay. The scarf was still tied round the lower part of her face, but I could see her eyes were open. They were dead, just two orbs of white with a black spot at their centre, looking at nothing, as if a living spark had been plucked out of her. As I got to her, Amy reached out and gently closed Emma's eyes.

"Joe!" Amy called.

Joe shuffled over. He was the only one who didn't

look devastated by the fact that Emma had died. He just looked puzzled.

"Is Emma all right?" he asked.

Amy nodded. "She will be now, Joe." She pointed at Emma. "Joe, you take her legs. Will, you get hold of her under her arms. Then follow me." To the others, she said: "You lot follow behind. And if we see a copper, just scarper and come back here."

Joe and I lifted Emma's body up. I was amazed how light she was. But then, she hardly ate anything. And she looked like she'd been small and thin to start with.

Amy led the way, and Joe and I carried Emma's body to the edge of the roof, and then started down the fire escape. Vicky, Paul and Mick followed. Out of the corner of my eye I saw Jim, still kneeling on the rooftop, writing slowly but carefully on the piece of cardboard.

We made it down the metal stairs of the fire escape. By the time we got to the bottom, Emma wasn't feeling so light any more. I was glad that Joe was there to take most of the weight.

We followed Amy as she led the way through back alleys and lanes until finally we came to a little square. At one side there was a tiny chapel. Not one of those grand places, but just a door in a wall, with a wooden sign outside that said "Gospel Hall".

"Put her down on the step here," said Amy.

Joe and I put Emma's body down on the step.

"Right," said Amy. "Gather round."

We were just gathering round Emma's body when we heard running footsteps, and for a moment I thought it was the police. But it was Jim. He hurried and joined us. In his hand he was holding the piece of cardboard.

"Sorry it took so long," he said.

Amy nodded, and Jim took his place amongst us, next to Joe.

"Bow your heads," said Amy.

We all bowed our heads.

"Dear God," said Amy. "This is Emma. She worked hard and was a good friend. She died too young because of life being cruel. Please take care of her in Heaven now she's dead, because she deserved better than she had."

Amy hesitated, as if she was going to say something more. Instead, she said simply in a whisper, so we could hardly hear her: "Amen."

"Amen," we all repeated.

We all straightened up.

"Right," said Amy. "Someone will find her here and look after her. We got to go. Come on."

As we all started to move away, Jim moved forward and put the piece of cardboard on Emma's body and tied it to the end of one of her apron strings. I could see there were words on it.

"What's it say?" I asked.

"Can't you read?" asked Jim.

I shook my head.

"No," I said. "I never learnt."

Jim pointed to the sign he'd made.

"It says, 'This is Em. She was poisoned by Lord Martwell and his match factory. May he rot in hell.'"

"You mustn't say that!" protested Vicky. "That's wrong!"

The rest of us looked at Amy, wondering what she thought. Amy shrugged.

"Emma dying was more wrong," she said. She nodded. "Leave it there, Jim. Maybe someone will take notice." She gave a deep heartfelt sigh as she looked at Emma's dead body one last time, then said, "Time to go."

Chapter twenty-four

The message that Jim left with Emma's body brought us big trouble. Whoever found her body and the piece of cardboard thought it was scandal and something ought to be done about it, and they put the story in the newspapers. The first we knew about it was when we were all on the roof about two days later, with Amy dividing the food up as usual, and six big men appeared from the fire escape. They looked tough. Three of them had broken noses, two had thick swollen ears, and each of them was carrying some sort of weapon. Five of them carried long hard cudgels, and one of them was swinging a wicked-looking length of chain from one fist. In his other hand he held a screwed-up newspaper.

"Right, you kids!" snarled the one with the chain. "Who did it?!"

We had all stood up and looked at them in alarm.

"Who did what?" asked Amy, but a sinking feeling in my stomach told me I knew what this was all about.

"Who put that sign on that dead girl?" raged Chain.

We all stared back at him and shook our heads, hoping we looked like we were telling the truth.

"We don't know any dead girl," said Jim.

Chain stomped over to Jim and stuffed the page from the newspaper down Jim's shirt-front.

"Yes you do!" he snarled. "She lived here! And don't lie! I've asked around and I know she lived here with you lot. Which means one of you put that sign on her. Who was it?"

And he waved the chain around viciously.

I felt sick. I knew what that length of chain could do to us. And the cudgels the other men were holding would break our bones with just one blow.

"Tell me!" he raged.

When we were still silent he reached out and grabbed hold of little Paul, who cried out in alarm.

"If you don't tell me who done it, I'm gonna start by breaking his arm!" he threatened.

Joe looked at Jim. He looked puzzled.

"It was—" he began.

"It was Billy," I said quickly, cutting Joe off.

Chain let go of Paul and came over to me.

"Billy?" he demanded.

I gulped and nodded.

"He was Emma's brother. He did it cos he was so upset."

"And where is this Billy?" demanded Chain.

I shook my head.

"He ran away," I said. "After he put her body down. He said

he couldn't bear to come up on this bit of roof again, where she'd died."

Chain glared at me, obviously weighing up what I'd told him, and whether I was lying. I held his stare and hoped I looked honest enough for him to believe me. Finally he spat on the ground and turned away from me and joined his five mates.

"All right," he said. "But that ain't the end of it. The gentleman what owns this building wants you off it. Now. You can walk off or we can throw you off. It's up to you. A few more dead kids don't matter one way or another. We get paid either way. What's it to be?"

The littlest kids, Vicky, Paul and Mick, looked as if they were about to burst into tears. Joe looked at Jim for guidance, who, in turn, looked at Amy. I saw anger fill Amy's face as she glared at Chain and the other thugs. Even though she was our leader, I blurted out: "We're going." Then I turned to Amy and added, apologetically, "Ain't that so, Amy?"

Amy hesitated, then nodded and said, "Yes."

To the others she said: "Gather up your things. We ain't coming back."

"Make sure you don't," snapped Chain. "If we see any of you again, we'll kill you. And don't believe we won't."

We gathered up our belongings from our sleeping places near the chimney stack, and tied them up into small bundles. All the while Chain watched us, the length of chain swinging from his hand, and the other men stood tapping the cudgels menacingly.

"Come on!" shouted Chain. "Hurry up, or I might forget we're letting you leave here alive!"

I only had the clothes I wore, so I helped Paul and Mick tie up their small bundles of belongings, while Amy helped Vicky and Jim helped Joe. Then we left, over the edge of the roof and down the fire escape. As we passed Chain and his men on our way to the fire escape, I tensed, expecting them to start beating us. But they didn't. They just stood there, Chain swinging that wicked length of chain and the others tapping their cudgels against their hands.

I was the last to leave. As I did, Chain suddenly flicked out with the edge of his palm, swiping me round the side of the head.

"And don't come back!" he warned.

Chapter twenty-five

We found ourselves a place to shelter for the night in a graveyard. It wasn't the best sort of place to be, and I could see that Vicky, Paul and Mick were looking at the gravestones unhappily, as if they expected the dead to come out. But it was safer than most places. We were all still worried that Chain and his gang might come after us. If they did, we were sure they'd look for us on the roofs.

"We'll find us another roof tomorrow," Amy said. "But tonight being here is safer."

Jim looked miserable.

"This is my fault," he said. "If I hadn't left that message on Em, we'd still be on our roof."

Amy shook her head.

"Lord Martwell's been threatening to kick us off that roof for ages," she said. "He give us a warning before, remember."

"Amy's right," I said. "That's why you thought I was a spy when I first met you all."

Jim sighed.

"It's still my fault," he said. "We might have had a bit longer."

"We'll be all right," said Amy confidently. "We always are, so long as we stick together."

Vicky gave another look round at the gravestones and shuddered.

"I don't like it here," she whimpered.

"Don't worry," said Amy reassuringly. "We'll get another roof tomorrow."

Jim reached into his shirt and pulled out the newspaper that Chain had stuffed down there.

"This is what got Lord Muck all riled up," he said. "We might as well see what it says."

He unfolded the sheet of newspaper and spread it out. He scanned the page, looking for the section where it said about Em.

"This is it," he said, stabbing his finger at the page. "'Girl Dead in Whitechapel. Industrialist accused. Yesterday a dead girl was found on the steps of Almond Street Gospel Hall in Whitechapel. On her body was a note accusing the noted factory owner, Lord Martwell, of being responsible for her death.

"'Lord Martwell told our reporter the dead girl was nothing to do with him. Whoever had written the note, this was a lie made up by troublemakers. Lord Martwell said conditions in his factory were as good as any others, and within the law.

"'When asked if he shouldn't be doing more to help the

poor, Lord Martwell said: "God made some people poor and some people rich. That is the natural order of things. It is God who has put people in their different places, some high and some low, and this must not be interfered with. Those people who talk about social reforms to help the poor are going against God's will.'" "

"God's will!" I echoed angrily. The thought that Lord Martwell blamed God for Emma's death made me see red. And then an idea came to me. An idea which would pay back Lord Martwell for what he'd done to Emma, and to us for getting his thugs to throw us off his roof.

"I'm going to burgle him," I said.

The others looked at me, their eyes and mouths open in shock.

"Burgle?" repeated Jim.

I nodded.

"You know I told you I used to be a chimney boy?" They nodded. "Well, I was a bit more than that. I worked as a climbing boy for a burglar." Hastily I added: "I didn't want to do it, but the man I worked for said he'd kill me if I didn't help him. So I used to climb up on the roofs of houses and get inside and let him in. Then we'd take stuff from inside the house."

"Burglary!" said Jim, horrified. "That's against the law!."

"I know," I said. "They caught me but I managed to get away." I still didn't tell them about my escape from

137

Newgate Prison, just in case one of them told someone else the story. Maybe Joe might say something, not meaning to tell on me, but just because he didn't know any better. And I was still an escaped prisoner.

"I said I'd never go burgling again," I continued. "But after what's happened to Emma, and to us, I think Lord Martwell deserves to get burgled and lose some of his precious money. We'll be able to go away and find somewhere better to live. Maybe get out to the countryside."

"Make a whole new start," nodded Jim thoughtfully.

The others were silent for a moment, thinking about it. Then Vicky said: "We could buy a proper headstone for Em. Put it in the churchyard, so people would know who she was."

Amy looked doubtful.

"I don't know," she said. "Say it goes wrong? Say you get caught?

I shrugged.

"They caught me once and I got away," I said.

I sounded confident, but inside I wasn't. Deep down I felt a sickness in my stomach at the thought of going into Lord Martwell's house and what would happen if I got caught. There'd be no escape from Newgate for me a second time. The prison warders would make sure of that. I'd be kept locked in a cell and possibly spend the rest of my life in prison doing hard labour. But the feeling of anger at someone like Lord Martwell saying what he did, and doing what he did, burned inside me like angry fire.

"Let me go with you," said Paul.

I looked at him, shocked.

"You?"

"Please," Paul pleaded. "I'm a good climber. I can climb with you. You might need help if anything goes wrong."

"No," I said firmly. "Climbing up a drainpipe for fun is one thing. Climbing up a drainpipe to carry out a robbery is very different. It's much more dangerous." I turned to the rest of them and said even more firmly, "When I do the job, none of you must be anywhere near it. If anything does go wrong and I get caught and you're seen near the place you'll be grabbed as well. Martwell's men saw us together. They'll say you were all part of the robbery."

Jim nodded.

"Will's right," he said. "We'd better stay out of his way."

"I'm still not sure it's right," said Amy uncertainly. "Burgling is wrong."

"Not against someone like Martwell," I argued. "Where does he make his money from? He steals it from girls like Emma by not paying them a proper wage. All we're doing is taking some of it back."

"It's not right," Amy said, shaking her head. "Robbery is robbery, whoever you do it to. It's wrong."

"What's our option?" asked Jim. "We starve on the streets,

being kicked off one roof after another. Then, like Em, we get sick and die one by one." He shook his head. "I'm with Will on this. We take what we can from Martwell. Just one job. Then no more."

Amy still looked doubtful. She sighed, and looked around at us other kids. I could tell what she was thinking. Me and her and Jim could look after ourselves. But Vicky, Paul and Mick needed looking after until they were older. And big Joe would always need someone to watch out for him.

Finally she nodded.

"OK," she said, but there was still that look of doubt and unhappiness on her face as she said it.

Chapter twenty-six

The next day Amy found us a new bit of roof to live on. It was on a factory that filled mattresses with straw, and there were rats running around all over the roof.

"It's only till we find a better roof," said Amy. "It'll be safe for us till then."

So we settled down and made a space for ourselves to sleep, and took turns to stay awake to keep the rats from running over us.

I started planning the burglary.

Because I was determined not to get caught, I spent time making sure there were few things to go wrong. The first thing to find out was where Martwell lived. Jim found that out for me. Martwell had two homes, a big one in the country and a house in town in Bloomsbury.

Once we'd found out about the Bloomsbury house, it was then a case of putting into practice what I'd learned from Hutch: talk to the servants who worked there and find out when Martwell was likely to be away. It was Amy who turned up trumps on this one. She got into conversation with one of the scullery maids who worked below stairs at the Bloomsbury house.

"Megs says at the moment Lady Martwell and the children are away at their big house in the country, and Lord Martwell's on his own there. But it turns out he often goes out gambling at some private club two nights a week. And he's going out tomorrow night. When that happens some of the servants go home as well. They take it in turns. Tomorrow night, the only servants who'll be in the house are the butler, the housekeeper and Megs, the scullery maid."

"Where do they sleep?" I asked.

"The butler and housekeeper and cook have rooms on the second floor," replied Amy. "The maids' rooms are at the top of the house, in the attic. Lord Martwell and his family are on the first floor."

"It would help if we had a plan of the inside of the house," I said. "Where the bedrooms are. Where the skylight comes in. That sort of thing."

"I've got that," said Jim, and he gave a proud smirk. "I had a long talk with the boy who works at the place they got most of their furniture. He had to carry a dressing table and some other stuff upstairs to the main bedroom."

Jim pulled a piece of paper from his pocket and unfolded it. He had made a drawing of the inside of the house and marked different rooms. Because I couldn't read, he pointed them out to me. "This is Lord Martwell's bedroom. This one is Lady Martwell's. These two are the children's. These two are guest rooms and are empty.

"These are the music room and the library, and other stuff." He moved his finger to the second floor. "These are the bedrooms Amy was talking about, where the butler and the top servants live. On the ground floor are the drawing room and the dining room and all the other rooms where they do their entertaining."

"What about doors to the outside?" I asked.

"Front door off the street goes into the hallway and the ground floor," said Jim, stabbing his finger at the drawing. "The back door comes out from the scullery at basement level."

I studied Jim's drawing and nodded thoughtfully. He'd done a great job in getting the information.

"Right," I said. "All I need now is a piece of cloth, a tin with some soft tar in it, and a bag."

"What do you want tar for?" asked Paul.

"Better you don't know," I told him.

I also needed a glass cutter, but I knew I wouldn't be able to get hold of one of those easily. My plan was to do my best to break the glass with a stone, and hope the cloth would muffle the sound.

"They're mending the road a few streets away," said Mick. "They've got tar there. I can get some for you. The roadmen give us bits to play with."

"Good," I said. "Right, here's the plan. I'll go in about midnight. The servants should be asleep by then. I'll do the job, get what I can, and meet you all back here. All right?"

"What if you get caught?" asked Jim.

"Then I won't be back," I said. "If I don't arrive back here by morning, get as far away from here as you can. I won't say anything about you, but Martwell's thugs might recognize me and come looking for you."

"You sure you can do this?" asked Amy.

I nodded, and forced a grin.

"Of course," I said. "I'm a climbing boy."

Chapter twenty-seven

I reached the alley that ran along the back of Martwell's house well before midnight, and found myself a doorstep in the shadows where I could hide and watch the place. I wanted to make sure there were no lights on when I went in, so I knew the servants would be in bed. I also wanted to make sure there was no one around in the streets nearby.

I must have sat there for about a quarter of an hour before I was sure that everything seemed clear.

I hurried across from the alley to the steps that went down to the cellar area. It struck me that so many of these big houses the posh people lived in were the same, which made it easier for burglars like me to rob them. Once you'd been in one big house, you knew what the layout of others would be like inside.

I got to the drainpipe, reached up and grabbed hold, and started my climb. Up, up, up I went. There were two sections of roof on Martwell's house. The first led to bedroom windows. Then there was another section of drainpipe that went right up to the top section of roof. That was where the skylights were, and that was where I was aiming for.

I got to the first section and grabbed hold of the iron guttering, and hauled myself up onto the sloping roof slates of the first section. I lay there for a bit, getting my breath back and listening, waiting to see if there was any sound from inside the bedroom windows.

I wasn't going to rush this job. I knew there were people inside the house and I didn't want to do anything or make any sound that would make them suspicious.

As I lay there on the slates, I heard a rustling sound. My ears pricked up and I was alert, like a fox. Was someone awake inside the house?

I realized the sound was coming from outside, from near the guttering! I looked, and saw Paul's face appear over the edge of the roof.

"I did it!" he whispered, and even in the darkness I could see the look of excitement and pride on his face. "I climbed all the way up!"

I was horrified.

"You shouldn't be here!" I whispered angrily at him.

Paul opened his mouth to say something, but I put my finger to my lips to shut him up. The last thing I wanted was people waking up because two boys were talking on the roof. Angrily, I gestured for him to go back down the drainpipe again, back to the ground. Paul's face crumpled into misery as I did this, the excitement that had been there a few seconds before vanishing. But he still didn't move.

I guess he was hoping I'd change my mind. I didn't. The last thing I wanted was Paul being caught and having that on my conscience. Once again I jerked my thumb downwards, then pointed at the edge of the roof where the drainpipe was, my expression firm and angry and showing him I meant it.

Paul looked really miserable. He gave a big sigh and turned back to the guttering, and then he slipped.

Whether he didn't have the proper shoes to get a grip on the roof slates, or whether he lost his balance for a second, I'll never know. All I know is he gave a yell as he disappeared over the edge of the roof.

I leapt forward, grabbing for him, and managed to catch hold of the sleeve of his jacket. The trouble was, leaping forward like that had taken me over the edge of the roof, and I only just managed to grab hold of the guttering with my other hand to stop us both from falling.

I hung from the gutter with one hand, Paul hanging suspended below me, my other hand gripping onto his jacket sleeve.

"Grab my legs!" I called. "Pull yourself up!"

I didn't care who heard me now. I didn't care if I was caught and arrested. All I cared about was saving Paul. There was a drop of about 30 feet below us.

"Come on, Paul!" I urged him. "Grab my legs!"

But Paul couldn't seem to get a hold. One of his arms was

trapped in the jacket sleeve I was holding, and the other was flailing wildly, getting hold of nothing.

"Swing towards the drainpipe!" I told him urgently. "Try and get your feet to grip that."

Paul swung towards the drainpipe, but we were just too far away from it.

The pain and pull on the one arm I was holding on with was terrible. My fingers that were gripping the iron gutter were going numb because of the weight pulling me down. Paul swinging below me just made that weight so much heavier.

"Climb up me, Paul, please!" I begged. "I can't hold on any longer!"

At last, I felt Paul's free hand grab hold of my trousers, getting a grip.

"Good!" I said. "Now climb up me!"

I thought that once Paul had climbed up me and got to the guttering, we could both work our way along it to the drainpipe. So far we were lucky: no one had appeared to find out what the noise was.

I gritted my teeth against the pain in my fingers holding onto the gutter. They felt like they were being torn apart.

"Come on, Paul!" I urged desperately.

And then the guttering broke.

Chapter twenty-eight

We fell. We didn't even have time to scream.

Paul hit the ground first with a sickening crunch, and I landed on top of him, my left arm smashing into the ground. I knew I'd broken it, I felt it crack. The pain was the worst I'd ever known.

I rolled off Paul, gritting my teeth against the pain in my arm.

"Come on, Paul!" I whispered.

But it was no use. He was dead. I could tell by the blank look in his eyes. The fall had been enough to kill him, but my landing on top of him had just made sure.

I felt sick. Not just from the pain of my broken arm, but because it was I who'd killed Paul. If I hadn't talked about being a climbing boy, and doing this burglary, Paul would still be alive.

I staggered to my feet. I looked down at Paul's dead body. There was nothing I could do for him.

No one had come running. I still had time to get away.

I staggered up the steps of the cellar area to the street, and then back to the shadows of the alleyways.

I couldn't go back to the other kids. I couldn't face them and tell them that Paul had been killed. They'd find out soon enough. But right now, as soon as Paul was found, there'd be trouble. The thugs would recognize Paul as one of the gang. If they found me with them, with a broken arm, they'd work out what had happened, and all the kids would be rounded up.

The best thing I could do for them was stay away. At least, until the hue and cry was over. Later, I'd find them and tell them what had happened. How Paul had died. But right now all I could do was hide somewhere until my arm felt good enough for me to move properly. Right now, the pain was making me feel sick.

A roof. That was the answer. I had to get to a roof where no one else was. I'd hide there. There was one roof that I knew about that no one lived on. This was the roof of a leather factory and the smell was awful because they had big tanks of urine where they soaked the animal hides to turn them into leather. The smell got into your nostrils and your clothes. No one would be up there. That's where I'd hide.

I stumbled along the alleyways and back lanes, holding my broken left arm to my side with my good hand, trying to fight off the dizziness and the pain. Two things filled my mind: getting to the roof of the leather factory, and Paul lying on the ground dead.

I don't know how long it took me. Time was a blur, and I can't even remember climbing the fire escape to the roof of the leather factory. But I did. Somehow I managed to crawl into a place between the chimneys and I lay down. I was shivering. Now I was here on the roof all I could see was Paul, his dead body twisted and lying at a funny angle, his face white and his eyes open. Paul was dead. And it was my fault.

I began to cry, and suddenly it was as if all the tears I'd ever held back in my whole life started to pour out of me, and I cried and howled. I cried for Paul, and for Em, the rest of the gang, and the pain in my arm, and for every rotten thing that had happened in my life.

The next day I woke up and I felt ill. Really ill. My arm was hurting. It felt like it had swollen to an enormous size. I guessed it had got poisoned in some way. Maybe the bone had torn into something inside me when it broke. I felt sick as well. And weak. There was a strange buzzing sound in my ears. I couldn't see properly because my eyes wouldn't focus.

I could hear sounds in the distance but I couldn't tell what they were. I felt freezing cold. Shivering. But at the same time I was hot. I could feel the sweat soaking into my clothes.

I'm going to die, I said to myself. I'm going to die, and then I'll be out of all this pain and misery. This'll be behind me then.

I wondered if this was how Em had felt before she died?

Paul. I could see Paul. Lying on the ground next to me.

His eyes were open. His face was dead white. All his bones were broken.

The pain in my arm filled me up.

I was dying.

Time passed. I don't know how long. Sometimes it was night, and sometimes it was day. All I knew was pain as I lay there hidden between those chimneys.

Then strangely, I felt someone touch me. There was a push, and then the pain in my arm tore through my body and I screamed out with the agony.

A man was bending over me, lifting me up, but he let me go when I screamed.

"Don't throw me off the roof!" I begged.

"Why would I do such a dreadful thing?" said the man.

"I can't move," I said. "My arm's broken." As the pain surged through my whole body from my broken arm again, I passed out.

Chapter twenty-nine

I woke up. I was in a bed. I'd never slept in a proper bed before. Not one like this, with white sheets and a pillow. It all smelled … clean.

I started to move, then felt something heavy pulling me down. I looked and saw that my left arm was covered in a thick, heavy plaster cast.

"He's awake," said a voice.

"I'll go and get Dr Tom," said another voice.

A boy appeared beside my bed and looked down at me. He was about my age. His clothes were ragged-looking, but clean. Another boy joined him. Then a third. They all stood looking at me.

"Where am I?" I asked. "Am I in Heaven?"

"No," said the first boy. "You're in the Boys' Home."

The Boys' Home? It sounded like a workhouse, like the Infant Asylum, but it didn't look or feel like a workhouse.

I looked around the room. There were lots and lots of beds, the same as the one I was in, along both walls. All of them had neatly folded white sheets on them.

There was the sound of footsteps, and then the man I'd

seen on the roof came over to my bed. He smiled down at me.

"So, our patient is awake," he said. "How does your arm feel?"

I nodded.

"It feels all right," I said.

"Good," he smiled.

I studied him, puzzled. His voice had an accent. Irish. Who was he, and what was this place? My bewilderment must have been obvious on my face, because he began to explain: "This place is a home for orphan boys who have nowhere else to stay," he said. "It's paid for by charitable donations given by people who think it's a disgrace that children should be sleeping in the streets. My name is Dr Tom Barnardo, but everyone here calls me Dr Tom. I assume I'm right in thinking you have no proper home?"

I nodded.

"That's right," I said.

"Then you'll have a home here," said Dr Tom. "Are you hungry?"

I nodded again.

"If you can get up and get yourself dressed with that arm in its plaster cast, we'll get some food inside you. If you can't, one of the other boys here will help you. Right, boys?"

The boys standing around my bed nodded.

"That's all right," I said. "I can dress myself." I had never

154

had anyone dress me since I was a baby, and I wasn't about to start now.

Dr Tom grinned and nodded.

"That's what I like to see," he said. "Independence of spirit." Turning to the boys again, he said: "In that case, boys, give our latest guest some room so he can get himself sorted out. Except for you, John. You stay here and bring the new boy down to the dining room when he's ready."

With that, they all trooped out of the room, leaving me with the boy called John.

Chapter thirty

And that was how I came to find a home at last.

I found out soon enough that Dr Tom was a young doctor who'd come to London from Dublin in Ireland. Soon after he arrived, he'd been shocked to discover so many children in London couldn't read or write and had had no education of any sort. So he started up a school for them. It was called a ragged school because it taught children whose clothes were ragged because they were poor, and most of them were homeless or orphans.

It was hearing the stories the children at the ragged school told him that made him realize how many hundreds of children lived on the streets of London, so he raised money and set up a safe place for them to stay. He set up a Home for Boys, and then later he set up a Home for Girls.

At these Homes boys and girls were given a comfortable place to live, food, and an education so they could be trained to get proper jobs.

As you can imagine, being at the Boys' Home was a bit of a shock at first, and I was very suspicious of the place, and of Dr Tom. But once I found out Dr Tom was genuine, I made it my job to try to find Amy, Jim, Joe, Vicky and Mick so they could come and live at the Home in safety, too.

It took me weeks to track them down, but I did. It was hard explaining to them what had happened to Paul. I expected them to be angry with me, but they weren't.

Jim, Joe and Mick joined me at the Boys' Home, and Amy and Vicky went to stay at the Girls' Home.

All that was sixteen years ago.

Now, I'm a young man of 25, and I work with Dr Tom helping run the Homes he's set up to house children in the poor parts of London. I learned to read and write and do sums, and I teach the new boys who arrive at the Homes. Quite a few of the Homes have been set up in London.

When I came here and I was asked my name, I made up a new last one. I called myself William Adams. I thought that way, if there were warrants still out for William Reed, burglar and escapee from Newgate Prison, I wouldn't get tracked down.

So that is who I am now. William Adams.

I never did find Vi's son, Norman Adams, but I thought taking his surname might help in some way. She was the first person who was ever good to me, before Dr Barnardo, so it seemed right and proper I should want her name as my own.

As for the rest, Amy and Vicky both got jobs as maids in big, posh houses. Jim did well with his education and joined the police force. Joe got a job lifting barrels on and off carts for a brewery. Mick found a place working in a shop that sold old clothes.

Lord Martwell got older and richer, and still parades around town in his finery. His match factory still produces matches, and workers with illnesses.

The main thing for me is I finally found somewhere I can live safely, and can help others. If I can stop one other young child going into a life of crime, like I was forced into, then I'm doing something useful with my life.

Historical note

Chimney boys and children in Victorian times

In 1840 an Act of Parliament was passed forbidding anyone under the age of 21 from climbing chimneys, and in 1864 Lord Shaftesbury introduced an Act imposing a fine on anyone breaking this rule. Despite this, the illegal practice continued, as can be seen from the fact that it was not until 1875 that Parliament passed an Act which stated that all chimney sweeps had to be licensed, and licences would only be issued to sweeps who did not use climbing boys.

Boys who cleaned chimneys were just one example of the harsh conditions of child labour in Victorian times. Others included young girls who worked in match factories, working long hours for poor pay and handling dangerous materials such as phosphorus, which caused a disease that rotted the lower jaw. Other jobs carried out by children included: sweeping roads and crossings, sewing sacks, clothes and shoes, and working in factories. For many children – especially the vast number of orphans and abandoned children – crime was their only way to get money: pickpocketing was rife, and climbing boys were in great demand as cat burglars.

In the poor areas of Victorian London, diseases such as cholera, typhoid, diphtheria, TB, scarlet fever, measles and polio killed thousands of children. In the 1830s half of all the funerals in London were for children under the age of 10. The major causes of much of the spread of disease in poor areas were overcrowding and poor hygiene, with drinking water containing raw sewage. In 1866 an outbreak of cholera swept through the East End of London, killing 3,000 people.

Crime and punishment in Victorian times
At the start of the nineteenth century there were over 200 capital crimes (crimes for which hanging was the punishment). In 1823 Sir Robert Peel's government reduced the number of capital offences by over 100, and from 1832 brought in various Parliamentary Bills to reduce the number even further. Shoplifting, sheep, cattle and horse stealing were removed from the list in 1832, followed by sacrilege, letter stealing, returning from transportation in 1834 and 1845, forgery and coining in 1836, and arson, burglary and theft from a dwelling house in 1837. By 1861 the number of capital crimes was reduced to four: murder, high treason, arson in a royal dockyard, and piracy.

Will's escape from Newgate Prison is based on a real event. In 1836 a chimney boy called Williams was sentenced to death by hanging for burglary. He escaped by climbing the wall of Newgate from the exercise yard, exactly as described. He climbed the 50-foot-high granite wall, and then clambered over the iron spikes, finally reaching the roof of the adjoining Press Yard Buildings. There, he managed to get help from sympathetic washerwomen, who tended the wounds he suffered from the spikes, and then let him out into the street.

Thomas Barnardo

Born in Dublin in 1845, in 1866 Barnardo arrived in London to train as a doctor, just before a cholera epidemic. In 1867, Barnardo set up a "ragged school" in the East End of London, where poor children could get a basic education. Ragged schools were set up in whatever space was available (railway arches, lofts, etc) to teach destitute and often homeless children reading, writing and arithmetic, along with bible study. The teachers were usually volunteer local people, and the money to run the schools came from charitable donations. Barnardo's encounters with poor children led him to discover the vast numbers of orphaned or abandoned children living destitute in London. In 1870 Barnardo opened his first Home for Boys in Stepney Causeway, which gave a home to destitute boys. He later opened the Girls' Village Home in Barkingside. By the time children left the Barnardo Homes they were able to make their own way in the world: the girls were equipped with domestic skills, and the boys learnt a trade.

Working children in the twenty-first century

Although Acts of Parliament were passed to prevent children from being exploited as labour in Britain, in many countries across the world children are still being used as workers, often in unhealthy or dangerous conditions.

250 million children aged 5–14 are working worldwide, and 126 million children work in hazardous conditions. In the Asia-Pacific Region, 122 million children work. In sub-Saharan Africa 26 per cent of children (49 million) work. Some children are working nine hours a day, seven days a week.

Most of these working children are in developing countries.

Children at risk today

In most of the nations of the developed world, legislation exists to protect children. But, despite this, every day new evidence surfaces of cruelty to children in the UK; not from work but from cruel and abusive adults. Sadly, for many children, their situation is just as bad in twenty-first-century Britain as it was for children in Victorian times.

There are organizations in the UK that exist to help children in extreme difficulties. These include Barnardo's, which is still active today, and the NSPCC (the National Society for the Prevention of Cruelty to Children).

www.barnardos.org.uk
www.nspcc.org.uk

Suggested further reading

Online:

A: for Victorian child chimney sweeps:

www.woodlands-junior.kent.sch.uk/victorians/children

www.bbc.co.uk/schools/primaryhistory/victorian_britain

www.victorianlondon.org/professions/chimneysweeps

B: for Dr Barnardo:

Wikipedia (the online encyclopedia)

www.biographybase.com/biography/Barnardo_Thomas_John

C: for Victorian child criminals:

www.nationalarchives.gov.uk/education/lessons

www.museumoflondon.org.uk

www.spartacus.schoolnet.co.uk/REVhistoryVIC2

Books:

Victorian child criminals:

The Victorian Underworld, Kellow Chesney (Pelican Books)

Also from Scholastic Children's Books:

Horrible Histories: Vile Victorians, Terry Deary

Horrible Histories: Villainous Victorians, Terry Deary

My Story: Crimea, Bryan Perrett

My Story: Mill Girl, Sue Reid

My Story: Workhouse, Pamela Oldfield

My Royal Story: Victoria, Anna Kirwan

My Story: Young Nanny, Frances Mary Hendry

Experience history first-hand with My Story –
a series of vividly imagined accounts of life in the past.

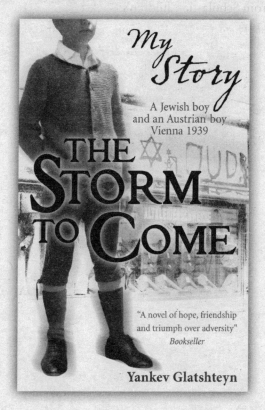

My Story

A Jewish boy
and an Austrian boy
Vienna 1939

THE
STORM
TO COME

"A novel of hope, friendship
and triumph over adversity".
Bookseller

Yankev Glatshteyn

Emil and Karl are best friends. Emil is a Jew;
Karl isn't. When three men take Karl's
mother away, who knows where, and the Nazis
murder Emil's father, the two boys find
themselves alone and scared, wandering in an
increasingly hostile city. Who can they trust
and where can they go...?

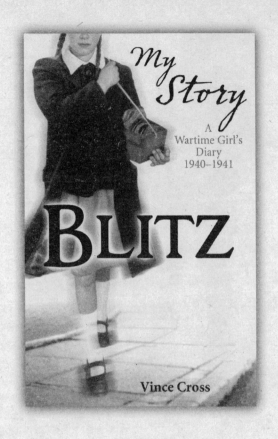

My Story

A
Wartime Girl's
Diary
1940–1941

BLITZ

Vince Cross

It's 1940 and with London under fire
Edie and her little brother are evacuated
to Wales. Miles from home and missing her family,
Edie is determined to be strong,
but when life in the countryside proves tougher than in
the capital she is torn between obeying her
parents and protecting her brother...

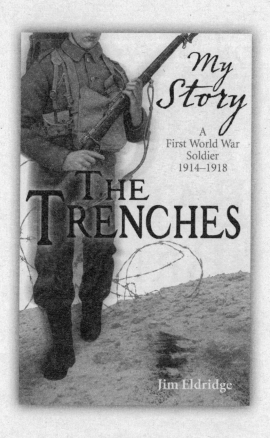

My Story

A
First World War
Soldier
1914–1918

THE TRENCHES

Jim Eldridge

It's 1917 and **Billy Stevens** is a telegraph
operator stationed near Ypres. **The Great War**
has been raging for three years when Billy finds
himself taking part in the deadly **Big Push** forward.
But he is shocked to discover that the **bullets**
of his **fellow soldiers** aren't just
aimed at the **enemy**...

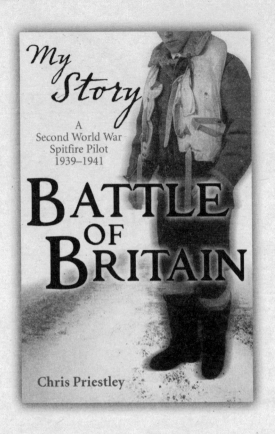

My
Story

A
Second World War
Spitfire Pilot
1939–1941

BATTLE
OF
BRITAIN

Chris Priestley

It's 1939 and Harry Woods is a
Spitfire pilot in the RAF. When his friend
Lenny loses his leg in a dogfight with the
Luftwaffe, Harry is determined to fight on.
That is, until his plane is hit and he finds
himself tumbling through the air
high above the English Channel...

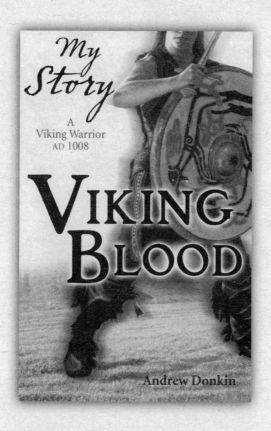

My
Story

A
Viking Warrior
AD 1008

VIKING
BLOOD

Andrew Donkin

It's AD 1008, and after being injured in a raid
that goes horribly wrong, Tor Scaldbane
is devastated at losing his chance to be a
legendary warrior.

But then he discovers the sagas of his ancestors: glorious,
bloody battles, ancient heroes, powerful gods ... and
realizes that all might not be lost after all...

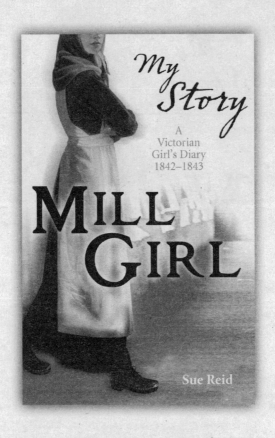

My Story

A
Victorian
Girl's Diary
1842–1843

MILL GIRL

Sue Reid

In spring 1842 Eliza is shocked when
she is sent to work in the Manchester cotton
mills – the noisy, suffocating mills. The work is
backbreaking and dangerous – and when she sees her
friends' lives wrecked by poverty, sickness
and unrest, Eliza realizes she must fight to escape
the fate of a mill girl...

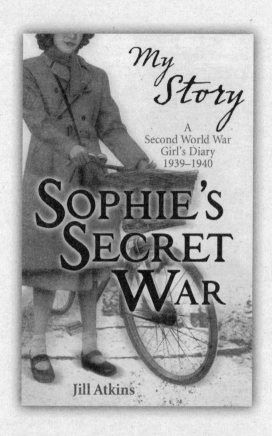

In 1939, the start of the Second World War,
Sophie becomes a messenger for a Resistance
group in Northern France. But as the
German invaders overwhelm the British forces
on the French coast, Sophie finds herself more
deeply involved with the Resistance – in a
dangerous plan to save a young Scottish soldier...

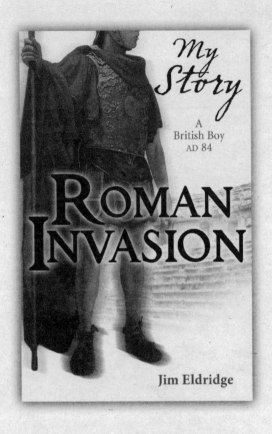

My Story

A
British Boy
AD 84

ROMAN INVASION

Jim Eldridge

It's AD 84 when Bran, a prince of the
Carvetii tribe, is captured by the Romans.
A legion of soldiers is marching east, to
build a military road. It's hostile
country, and Bran is to go with them as a
hostage to ensure the legion's safety ... but
no one is safe in newly conquered Britain.